Loving Ben

Loving Ben

—

ELIZABETH LAIRD

**Delacorte
Press**

Published by
Delacorte Press
Bantam Doubleday Dell Publishing Group, Inc.
666 Fifth Avenue
New York, New York 10103

This work was originally published in Great Britain by William
Heinemann Ltd. as *Red Sky in the Morning.*

Design by Richard Oriolo

Library of Congress Cataloging in Publication Data

Laird, Elizabeth.
  Loving Ben / Elizabeth Laird.
    p.   cm.
  Summary: Anna's teen years bring maturity and fulfillment as
she experiences the birth and death of a loved and loving
hydrocephalic brother, changing ideas about character in both
boyfriends and girlfriends, and working with a child with
Down's syndrome.
  ISBN 0-385-29810-2
  [1. Brothers—Fiction.   2. Death—Fiction.   3. Hydrocephalus
—Fiction.   4. Down's syndrome—Fiction.   5. Handicapped—
Fiction.]
  I. Title.
PZ7.L1579Lo   1989
[Fic]—dc19   89-1534
                                                       CIP
                                                        AC

Manufactured in the United States of America
October 1989
10 9 8 7 6 5 4 3 2 1
BG

For Graham, Margaret, and Janet

One

As long as I live, I shall never forget the night my brother was born. For one thing, I didn't get a wink of sleep. I'd only been in bed a few minutes when I heard Dad talking on the telephone. My bedroom's pretty small, and if I lean out of bed far enough, I can open the door without actually getting out of bed, so I did, and I heard Dad say, "That's right, the second house on the left past the shops. And please hurry."

His voice sounded so urgent, I guessed at once he must be calling the ambulance, and I knew my time had come. Well, it was Mom's time really, but mine too, in a way, because I was going to be in charge while she was away. I'd practiced everything in my mind, so I just got calmly out of bed and put on my dressing gown and groped around for my glasses. Then I went calmly out of the room and walked down the hall to Mom and Dad's bedroom. I didn't even run.

"Now just relax, Mom," I said. "Everything's under control." I must have said it too calmly, because no one took any notice. Mom's face was screwed up, and Dad was looking at her, standing quite still, with one leg in his trousers and the other out. He looked perfectly ridiculous. Then Mom's face went ordinary again, and she turned her head and saw me, and she looked quite normal. In fact, she gave me a smile. Then Dad started pulling on his trousers again. It was like starting up a video again after a freeze frame.

After that everything I'd planned to say was swept out of my head, because things happened too fast. Mom's face screwed up again, and she started taking loud, rasping breaths. I've never seen such an awful look in anyone's eyes, not even in a war film.

Dad grabbed his jacket and pushed past me out of the room. Then I suppose he must have realized it was me, because he came back and ruffled my hair the way he does when he wants to be nice to me. I hate it, but I don't like hurting his feelings, so I just suffer in silence.

"Be a nice girl," he said. "Go and get me a cup of tea. The ambulance won't be here for another five minutes. I've got to go and phone your granny."

I couldn't believe it. I've never heard anything so callous in all my life. There was his wife, probably dying, in the most awful agony, trying to give birth to his own child, and all he could think of were his own selfish pleasures. I realized how woman has suffered from man's selfishness since time began.

"Sorry, Dad," I said with dignity. "I expect Mom needs me. You'll find the tea in the usual place."

But then Mom gave an awful scream, and Dad rushed back into the bedroom and shut the door in my face. I didn't dare go in. I didn't even want to anymore. I felt too small and helpless. Frightful thoughts rushed through my mind, like what would happen if Mom died and I had to sacrifice my youth to look after Dad and bring up Katy, who was seven and absolutely horrible.

The minute I thought of Katy, I remembered my responsibilities. It was my job to run the house and family while Mom was otherwise engaged, and I decided I had better start by running Katy. I went back down the corridor to her room.

Katy is an unusually irritating child. Even Mom admits that she's a nuisance. She says it's because Katy's going through a stage, but either Mom's wrong or else it's a very long stage, because Katy seems to have been in it since she was born. One of the worst things about her is that you can never get her to go to sleep. We all have to creep around the house once she's gone to bed, and I can't even play my own tapes in my own room, which I feel, quite frankly, is a violation of my human rights. And she wakes up in the middle of the night if a moth so much as brushes its wings against her bedroom window. I never would have thought she'd sleep through the noise Mom was making, but that's the maddening thing about Katy. She's so unpredictable. There wasn't a sound coming from her room. I knelt down and looked through the keyhole. She always has a night-light on because she thinks she's so delicious that witches are just dying to come and eat her in the night, so I could see clearly enough that she was fast asleep.

"Well," I thought, "that gives me one less thing to worry about," but at the same time I almost wished Katy had been awake, because I didn't have anything to do. I certainly wasn't intending to betray Mom by making Dad a cup of tea.

Then I realized that I could at least phone Granny, which Dad seemed to have forgotten about, so I went downstairs to the phone in the hall and was just beginning to dial when the doorbell rang. The ambulance had come.

There were only two ambulancemen but they filled up our small downstairs hall completely. It's so narrow that if two people meet, one of them has to turn sideways and stand against the wall while the other squashes past. I used to think of ways of making sure it wasn't me who had to stand against the wall, like pretending, if I was holding something, that it was very heavy, or being in a hurry to use the bathroom, but I stopped all that kind of childish stuff years ago. Still, I've never stopped minding that our hall is so shabby and small, not like Debbie's (she used to be my best friend), and suddenly I got worried about it.

How would they get Mom down the stairs on a stretcher? Supposing it stuck, like that time when Dad was fitting shelves in their bedroom and he and Mom were trying to get the old wardrobe down the stairs? It got completely wedged between the wall and the banisters, and Dad had to get a saw and cut it in half before it took off any more wallpaper. He was furious, and it took hours to free the wardrobe. But Mom didn't have hours. If she got stuck on her stretcher, she'd have to have the baby right there on the stairs.

As it happened, Mom didn't need a stretcher at all. Dad came out of the bedroom, looking pale and shaky

4

and awful, and the men ran upstairs, and then one rushed out again and said, "Where's the telephone, love?"

And he dialed, and when I heard him talking, I started to feel trembly myself and sick.

"This is Alan here," he said. "I've got an emergency over on Blythe Road. Lady in labor. Too far gone to get her to hospital. She's started pushing, and the baby's almost there. Stan's doing what he can, but he says it's not looking quite right. Best get a doctor over here quick. We've got the oxygen and stuff, but we haven't got the whole neonatal kit if they need to do full resuscitation."

He must have forgotten about me, because he started off up the stairs again when he'd put the receiver down. I couldn't bear to let him go. I had to know what was going on.

"Is . . . is everything all right?" I asked. It sounded more feeble than I'd meant it to, but I didn't know what to say. I was frightened.

"Course it is," he said. He was using that awful cheerful voice they use to children when they want to deceive them. "Just a precaution. Your Mommy's going to be fine. So's the baby, I expect. It all happened just a bit too quick, that's all."

He patted my shoulder just as if he'd been a relative. I was only twelve then, but I was mature for my age, and it was not surprising that I felt offended.

"I'm quite prepared to give blood if necessary," I said. The idea made me feel sick, but if Mom needed my blood, there was naturally no more to be said. He had the nerve to laugh.

"Oh, we won't need your blood," he said. "Best thing you can do is be a good girl and keep out of the way. Tell you what, do you know how to make a cup of tea? Why don't you put the kettle on, then? Me and Stan could use some when we've finished with this."

If he hadn't put it like that, of course, I wouldn't have dreamed of making a cup of tea. But I knew that if I didn't, he'd think I didn't know how to, so I went to the kitchen and filled up the kettle. But all the time it was boiling, and while I was putting mugs and milk and sugar on the tray, I kept thinking about Mom and the baby.

Up until then I hadn't thought about the baby much as a real person. Quite honestly, I'd been shocked when Mom told me she was pregnant. I couldn't imagine her and Dad having sex. The whole idea seemed disgusting. Especially in our own house. Their bedroom didn't look right for it. It was too ordinary. But I'd gotten used to her getting bigger and being tired and relying on me more for things. In some ways I'd enjoyed it. I'd gotten quite good at doing a stir-fry for dinner and heating up pizzas in the oven. I could even do lamb chops and two vegetables, though it took hours to peel the potatoes.

Somehow, though, I hadn't thought much about the baby. I'd wanted a brother, I knew that much, mainly because I didn't want another Katy around the place, and I'd started knitting a cardigan, but I'm not much good at knitting, so I'd pulled it undone and tried to learn to crochet instead. But it got in a tangle, so I never managed to get anything finished. Dad had gotten the baby carriage down out of the attic, and Mom had lined the crib again in some new flowery material. It looked pretty, waiting there all clean and empty, beside her bed, but I hadn't been able to imagine a real, live baby in it.

Then I remembered something I'd read about in a Victorian novel. Grandma's got a whole stack of them that she used to read, about a hundred and fifty years ago. They have titles like *Lost in London* and *Little Faith*, and they're all horribly sad and religious. The children go around barefoot in the snow selling matches, and their mothers are gin-sodden, and the babies die, and when you read them, you cry and cry. I even got sinusitis once because I cried so much over *Christie's Old Organ*. But I like them too. After I've read one, I feel pure, and refined, and ready to face death.

Anyway, when babies are born in those old books, the mother's poor eldest daughter is always sent to the kitchen to boil gallons of water. It never explained what the water was for, but I knew that was the right thing to do. So I got out the pressure cooker and the biggest pots I could find and filled them up and turned on every burner on the stove. I slopped a bit on the floor, but I managed all right.

It took quite a long time, finding everything and filling them up, and I was still at work when Dr. Randall came. He went up the stairs two at a time, and then another ambulance came, and the men took this funny box thing upstairs. After a while they came down again, holding it carefully, and drove away. The doctor was still there. I could hear him in Mom and Dad's bedroom, which is right above the kitchen. But the rest of the house was quiet. Then I realized that the first ambulancemen, Alan and Stan, had gone too, and they hadn't even bothered to have their cup of tea. I knew then for certain that they'd just been humoring me and trying to keep me out of the way. Typical!

It was so quiet upstairs that I began to feel a bit worried. What could they all be doing? Was Mom all right? And shouldn't the baby be crying? Mom had promised that I'd be the first after Dad to see it, but no one had called me. I wanted desperately to know what was going on. But I felt too scared to go up and open the bedroom door and just walk in. Medical things seem kind of holy to me. Bursting in on the doctor doing something would be as bad as jumping up in church and shouting "Hi there!" to the minister.

Then I remembered the tea. Surely everyone would really and truly want a cup of tea by this time. After all, it was practically morning. The kitchen window was filling with a sort of grayish light, and there were red streaks across the sky. I'd never seen the dawn before. It was eerie and grand. Suitable for a birth, really. I checked that I'd put out enough mugs, filled the teapot (the kettle had boiled ages ago), and staggered upstairs with the tray. Then I put it down and opened the door a crack and picked it up and went in, holding the tray in front of me so that it would be the first thing they all saw.

I could see at once that they'd been having a very deep conversation. Mom was lying back in bed looking white and tired, and Dad was sitting beside her holding one of her hands. Dr. Randall was on the other side of the bed looking serious. Mom saw me first.

"Oh, Annie!" she said, and gave a wobbly kind of

laugh, and then Dad jumped up and came toward me and made a big fuss about taking the tray. I wasn't fooled. I knew he was trying to keep me from seeing Mom cry. I knew quite well that that was what she was doing.

"Where is it? Is it a boy? Can't I see him yet?" I whispered to Dad.

He just stood there, not saying anything. Then he turned, with the tray in his hands, and looked over to Dr. Randall, and Dr. Randall came toward me and said in that stupid voice grown-ups never use to each other, "Yes, Anna, you've got a dear little brother, but he's not very well, and we've had to take him to the hospital."

"That box," I whispered. Somehow I couldn't bring myself to speak normally. "He was in that box, wasn't he? Is he . . . ?"

Dr. Randall smiled for the first time.

"No, he's not dead, Anna. That was only an incubator. It's a special box for babies that need extra warmth and attention. He's not going to die. But . . ."

Now it was his turn to stop and look at Dad, and this time Dad was great. He just put his hands on my shoulders.

"Your brother's not quite right," he said. "Dr. Randall thinks he may be handicapped. We won't be able to tell yet, for a week or two, but it doesn't look . . ." and then the worst possible thing happened. Dad actually cried. He didn't sob or anything. He just crumpled up a bit.

That set me off, of course. I've never been able not to cry if someone else is. It's infectious, like giggling or yawning or something. And then Mom started, and we were all crying, and I felt really sad, but one horrible part of me was looking on from outside and thinking, Well, well. Fancy Mom and Dad and me all crying together over a serious family matter, and Katy still being asleep. That makes me feel really one of them.

I still couldn't imagine the baby. I knew with my brain that it was sad, him being handicapped, but I couldn't really feel it, if you know what I mean.

It's funny how you feel when you stop crying, if you've been crying with someone else. It's embarrassing, of course, but quite comfortable, too, in a way. You feel loving and close together, and empty, too.

After a bit, I began to think awful thoughts. What did handicapped mean? Would he look funny? Would he have those Oriental eyes some babies have? Would his legs and arms jerk a lot? Somehow, because we'd all been crying together, I felt especially daring, so I came right out with it to Dr. Randall.

"What do you mean, 'handicapped'?" I said.

Dr. Randall shook his head.

"I was just telling your parents, Anna," he said. "We don't know yet. We'll have to wait and see."

"Yes, but will he be blind, or deaf?" I asked.

Mom and Dad were sitting in a specially still kind of way, and I knew they were dying for the answer, too. Dr. Randall looked more cheerful.

"Oh no, I'm sure he'll be able to see and hear all right," he said.

"Will he look nice, or will he look funny and dribble

and all that?" I asked. It sounds awful, but I cared about that more than anything.

"I don't know, Anna," Dr. Randall said. "I honestly don't know. But all babies are very sweet, you know, even when they're . . ." He stopped.

"Can't you even tell us," I said, "if he'll be able to play, and go to school, and talk, and laugh, and everything?"

The cheerful look wiped itself off Dr. Randall's face.

"He'll be able to laugh," he said slowly. "Oh yes, I'm sure he'll laugh. But for the rest, let's wait and see, shall we? I think we all need some sleep now." He patted Mom's hand.

"You should try to rest," he said. "I'm sure you're very tired. You've done well to manage a home delivery with a birth of this kind. Quite unusual, in fact. I've given you a good strong dose. Make the most of it. You can phone the hospital anytime, but there won't be any news until tomorrow morning. The nurse will be here to help you at breakfast time. And try not to worry. He's quite stable, you know. There's no danger."

He picked up his bag and clicked it shut. He seemed suddenly in a hurry to go. The strain, I suppose. Mom always says that emotional upsets are more exhausting than anything else. Still, he didn't have much to upset him. It wasn't *his* baby that wasn't going to run about. All in the day's work for him, I should think.

He'd only been gone half a minute when he poked his head around the door again.

"There seems to be rather a lot of steam coming out of the kitchen," he said.

Steam! Boiling water! Of course! I'd left the four burners on full blast. I jumped up like a startled rabbit and squeezed past Dr. Randall and was in the kitchen in a flash. There was so much steam, I could hardly see the cooker. Fortunately none of the pots had boiled dry, but the walls were streaming with water. I felt like such a fool. I was afraid they'd laugh at me. Dr. Randall had never even mentioned needing any boiling water. I decided I'd try to empty all the pots and clean up quickly before Dad came down and saw, and then I could say that in my excitement I'd left the kettle on. But it was too late. Dad came into the kitchen right behind me.

"Very sensible, Spanner," he said in a matter-of-fact voice. He's always calling me silly names that rhyme with Anna. It drives me crazy sometimes, especially if he forgets and does it in front of other people. It sounds so weird. But he won't stop. He just laughs and says, "You know what they say, 'A loved child has many names,' so you be grateful, Gloriana."

I was relieved, anyway, that he didn't laugh.

"Well," I said, "I know boiling water is the right thing to do when a baby's born, but quite honestly, I don't know what it's for."

Dad didn't seem very sure either.

"Oh, sterilizing instruments or something, I suppose," he said vaguely. "Anyway, we'd better go to bed now. There's not much of tonight left."

But I didn't feel tired at all. Not yet, anyway. I knew I'd feel awful the next day. But just now there were too many things I wanted to know.

"Does it always hurt that bad?" I blurted out. I hadn't meant to ask Dad that, but I couldn't help myself.

"Does what hurt?" he said. I excused him for being so thick and insensitive on the grounds that he was an ignorant male and didn't know any better.

"Having a baby, of course," I said. "Mom's face, and then the way she screamed. . . ."

"You'll have to ask her," he said. "I wouldn't know, would I? But Mom seems to think it's worth it. It's how you and Kate were born, after all."

"And now you've got a son, too," I said, and then I wished I hadn't said it, because Dad looked very sad.

"Yes," he said. "And now I've got a son. Come on, Susanna. It's bedtime."

Two

———

I FELT PRETTY FUNNY GOING TO SCHOOL THE NEXT MORNING, partly because I was completely exhausted, I suppose. Dad said I could stay home if I liked. He'd gotten the week off from work. But I wanted to go. One reason was to get out of the house, because there was an awfully gloomy atmosphere, and Mom cried a lot, and Dad was on the phone all the time. Katy was a pest too. She'd gotten it into her head to be all fluffy and sugar-sweet and babyish, and I could have kicked her.

The other reason was that I was bursting to tell everyone at school. It's not often that I have some real news. Not like Sandra, whose older brother is in the Marines, or Miranda, who goes to tons of discos and does things with boys. Actually I'm not all that popular at school. I used to be best friends with Debbie, ages ago, and that was fine, because everyone likes her, so they let me into their group, too.

Debbie's one of the most beautiful people I've ever seen. She's got this wonderful deep chestnut hair that she can flick about her face and it falls back into place, like on the shampoo ads. And she's got a long, finely chiseled nose and perfectly even teeth and transparent skin covered with a sort of bloom, like a peach, and huge luscious eyes that are big and brown like a spaniel's. It sounds corny, but it's true. I can gaze at Debbie for hours. It's not that I'm in love with her, or anything peculiar like that. I don't even like her anymore since she started going off with Emma, who laughs at me behind my back and calls me a health hazard because of my acne. I just like beautiful things, that's all. I've got a strong aesthetic sense. And looking at Debbie is like looking at a perfect work of art.

Ever since I knew Mom was pregnant, I'd been planning my announcement at school, so I couldn't bear to put it off. And it was lovely. Even better than I'd hoped. Everyone was fascinated.

I told it really dramatically. Well, it was dramatic, after all. It's not every baby that's born at home because it all happened too quickly for the mother to get to the hospital. And then there were two ambulances, one arriving after the other, and the doctor, and me knowing how to boil up lots of water, and the doctor telling me how sensible that was (well, it was Dad really, but I cheated on that bit). They loved the bit where I saw them carrying in that little box, and my dreadful premonition that something was terribly wrong, and how I'd stood, rooted to the spot in the hall, with my hand over my pounding heart, trying to pray. And then there was the relief when Dr. Randall said it was only an incubator. But somehow I couldn't tell anyone that he might be handicapped. I couldn't quite admit it to myself yet.

"I wonder what he looks like," said Debbie. "It's too bad you didn't even get a glimpse, Anna. I bet he's got those lovely little hands and feet that babies always have. I do love babies."

"I bet his front teeth stick out like his big sister's do," said Emma with a nasty snigger. I ignored her. I could see she was only jealous and afraid that Debbie might start being my friend again. And for once, Debbie took my side. I'll say this for her, when she's decided to be nice to you, she's really lovely.

"Don't be silly, Em," she said. "Newborn babies haven't got any teeth. Anyway, Anna's teeth are going back in now with that brace thing. I bet he's sweet, Anna. Can we come over when he's back home and see him?"

I felt a sudden chill, like when you know you haven't done the right homework and it's got to be handed in.

"I don't know. I'll have to ask Mom," I said. "He's quite delicate, Dr. Randall says. He's got to be protected from any possible source of infection." I looked hard at Emma when I said that. She's more of a health hazard than me. She never stops eating sweets, and the fur sticks out half an inch on her teeth.

They sort of drifted off after that. All except Vicky. She's the one in our class none of us can stand. She never gets picked for team games, and no one likes sitting next to her. I do try to be nice to Vicky, or at least not actively nasty. I know how awful it is not to be liked. But I'm not desperate enough for a friend to go around with her. I mean, there are limits.

That evening we had a long discussion about the baby's name. Before he was born, Dad had decided on Edward. He said it sounded strong and silent and reliable. Mom wanted James. She said she'd always promised her dad that if she ever had a son, she'd call him after his granddad. I wanted something a bit more up-to-date, like Jason or Jasper.

Katy and I were in Mom's bedroom when Katy brought the subject up.

"Let's call him Sam," she said. "Oh, please, darling Mommee, plee-eese."

She was using the same whiny voice she puts on when she wants to get a Mars bar out of someone. That child has no sense of occasion. Anyway, she only likes the name Sam because her best friend Tracey's older brother is called Sam. Katy thinks she's in love with him. In love! At seven years old! I ask you.

"I know," I said. "Why don't we give him four names? Princes have four names. He could be James Edward Jasper Sam, then we'd all be happy."

"No!" said Mom suddenly and sharply. "Not James!"

"But I thought you said you'd promised . . ." I began, but I looked at her face and thought better of it. I seemed to be getting into deep water without quite knowing why.

Dad came in then, with a cup of tea for Mom.

"Talking about names, are you?" he said. "Well, I've made a decision. I'm his dad, and I've got the last word. We're going to call him Benedict. I've looked it up. It means 'blessed.' "

I saw him look at Mom, but she turned her face away.

"Benedict." I turned it over in my mind and began to like it. Ben. Benny. Benedict.

"Benedict what?" I said. "What's his middle name?"

"Just Benedict," said Dad. "I don't think he'll need another name."

He paused, but Mom didn't say anything.

"Well, that's decided then," said Dad, and he took the empty tray away again.

I was at school when Mom and Dad brought Ben home from the hospital. I could tell at once that something exciting had happened when I opened the front door. I sometimes think I must have special powers. I'm probably psychic, and I'd make a great witch or a medium or something. But I wouldn't dream of getting mixed up with all that stuff. I'm too sensible. After all, you never know what kind of horrors that sort of thing can lead to.

Actually it might have been the smell that gave me the clue. There was a faint waft of baby on the air, that powdery, milky, soft smell that they only have for the first few months. A great wave of excitement rushed over me, and I dropped my bag and tore off my jacket and raced upstairs.

Mom was just settling him down to sleep. She looked much happier than she had for the last few days. She'd been so miserable and snappy and weepy. I'd had a horrible feeling that she might just leave Ben at the hospital and never bring him home. I felt dreadfully afraid that she wouldn't love him. And if she didn't love Ben, perhaps she would stop loving me, too. But when I saw the tenderness on her face, I felt such relief I could have danced all around the room. I felt as if she'd been a long, long way away and had come home again.

"Come and see him, Annie," she said.

I sometimes wonder if I would have loved Ben quite so much if Mom hadn't shown me his feet first. She lifted up the edge of his coverlet, and I saw his tiny, perfect miniature toes, pink as shells, soft as petals. He must have felt the coverlet move, because he stretched them out and then curled them up again. I hadn't ever seen anything so beautiful in my whole life.

Then Mom put the coverlet back and pulled down the other end, and I saw him, my little darling brother, for the first time. His eyes were shut, but his mouth was still moving. It was sucking a bit, in and out. I could see at once that something was wrong with him. His head was far too big. The veins in it stuck out too much and looked too blue. But beside each lovely little ear, a curl of hair grew outward, corkscrewing out from his head, perfect and silky and fine. I put out my hand to touch.

"Can I, Mom?" I said.

"Yes, of course." She was smiling, but in that wobbly kind of way that meant she was nearly crying too. She bent down and picked his diaper off the floor and went off with it to the bathroom, and I was alone with Ben.

I may have been only twelve and nearsighted and pimply, but I knew how to fall in love. I fell in love with Ben at that moment.

"I don't care how handicapped you are," I whispered to him. "I love you. I'll always love you. I'll protect you and look after you. If anyone's going to be mean to you, they'll have to deal with me first."

I bent over the crib and kissed him. It was like kissing a rose. He moved a bit, and I felt he'd heard me. It was silly, of course. He couldn't possibly understand, or know who I was, or even feel much at his age. He didn't even have his eyes open. But I felt as if he loved me, too.

I think the few weeks after that were the happiest of my life. I no longer cared what anyone said or did to me at school. I just lived for the moment when I could get home, race up to Mom's bedroom, pick Ben up, and give him a huge cuddle. I hardly noticed that his big head was growing bigger and bigger and that his poor little neck was too weak to hold it up. I was too busy fussing over his diaper and powdering his little bottom. Mom laughed at me.

"You'll make a wonderful mother yourself one day," she said.

What do you mean, "one day"? I thought scornfully. I'd make a wonderful mother now. Apart from breast-feeding—I couldn't do that, of course—I felt as if I could do everything else for Ben. I could dress him and bathe him and rock him to sleep, and take him for walks in his carriage.

"I notice you're not so keen on dealing with his dirty diapers or washing his clothes," Mom said dryly. But I knew I could do all that if I had to. In fact, I even daydreamed sometimes (I knew it was wrong, but I couldn't help it) that something had happened to Mom and Dad and I really was in charge of Ben, all by myself.

Maybe it wouldn't have been so great. Maybe I'd have gotten bored and lonely and worried and fed up. But for a couple of hours after school every day it was perfect.

Actually, after a while real life asserted itself again.. It wasn't that I loved Ben any less, it was just that I had other things to worry about—like exams. They're quite easygoing at my school, really, but at the end of the summer term every year the whole place suddenly goes berserk. They load us up with work and make us completely neurotic. I think it's sadistic, really, to have exams in June, when we get the only decent weather we're likely to have for the whole year. I mean, what's wrong with November, when no one's got anything better to do? I blame the teachers. I'm sure they make us do exams in June so they can have an easy time just supervising us and dreaming about the vacations they're going to have in the country or the Bahamas or somewhere. It's all right for some.

I don't know why I mind so much about exams. They scare me stiff. I think it's dreading the moment when the teacher reads the marks out and everyone knows whether you're one of the worst or one of the best. And the trouble with being so scared is that it stops me from learning anything. My mind goes numb. I mean, how can you do brilliantly with a numb mind? And some of the exams are completely pointless. What's the idea of an art exam? You're either a genius or you aren't. And to find out which you are, they might just as well look at the last creation you did in class. I suppose they've got what Dad calls the bureaucratic mentality.

Anyway, I worked very hard that term and didn't do

too badly. Debbie was top in history as usual, and nearly top in geography, but I beat her in French and English. *Très bien pour moi.*

Partly because of exams and partly because of Debbie going off with Emma, I didn't have much social life that summer. I suppose, though, if I'm honest with myself, the real reason was Ben. I told Mom I wanted to have him all to myself, and I didn't see why I should have to share him with anyone else, but I know that it was really because I didn't want them to see him. I think Mom realized. She didn't push me into asking anyone over anyway, not even on my birthday. Actually, she wasn't seeing some of her old friends much either. I noticed she kept to the house quite a lot and didn't go out very often. Perhaps it was just having a small baby. But I don't think it was only that.

It was quite obvious to everyone after a few months that Ben was very badly handicapped. His head was twice as big as it should have been. "Hydrocephalus," the doctor called it. He said they'd be able to operate later, to take some of the fluid out of his head, so that it would be smaller, but it wouldn't make any difference to the handicap. We must never hope he'd grow up normal.

"Severe mental and physical retardation," it said on a letter Mom got from the hospital. You don't have to be a medical genius to know that means bad news. Somehow it didn't make me love Ben any less. It made me love him more. It made me want to shield him from anyone who didn't understand, who might laugh at him, or be embarrassed by him or look down on him.

Three

———

For the next two years I lived what they call a double life. It sounds romantic when you put it like that, but it was really an awful worry. Home and school were completely separated, or as separated as I could make them. If I ever become an actress, I shall owe my talent to the training of those years. I used to shut the front door every morning playing the part of Dad's Hosanna, or whatever nickname he gave me that day, and the light of Ben's life, and somewhere between the garden gate and the bus stop I'd become pimply Anna Peacock (Pee-wit the Pea-brain), the dummy of the eighth grade.

For a long time I didn't mind too much about school. I lived in a dream world, divorced from the realities of everyday life. The awful truth is that I was madly in love with Miss Winter. She had a slim body and short curly hair, and when she slammed the ball over the net in tennis lessons, her shorts sort of flipped up and settled down again on her iron-hard thighs, and I used to feel a dreadful yearning to be saved from a man-eating shark by her. Too embarrassing to remember, really. Having a crush on Miss Winter didn't do me any good, either. I went all numb, and I just let myself in for unnecessary suffering. I still wince at the memory of her shouting at me,

"*Run,* Anna! Where are your arms? For heaven's sake, girl! Hit the ball! Harder! Are you paralyzed or something?"

It would have been much more sensible to fall in love with Miss Penny, because English is my best subject, and she liked me as well. But there you are. Love is blind. And it's hard to take a person seriously when their nickname is Spenda. Spenda Penny. Get it? Anyway, all that kind of thing is far behind me now, I'm glad to say. I grew out of it months ago.

At home I was a different person. I belonged to Ben. By the time he was two, he had grown quite big, and his head, of course, was enormous. I knew he wasn't developing in the way that most babies do. I mean, he didn't learn to sit up till he was nearly a year old, and he was only just crawling on his second birthday. I could remember Katy, when she was two, putting shapes into a plastic letter-box thing and stacking up a tower of plastic pots. Mom hadn't even gotten them out for Ben. I went up to the attic and brought them down one day. I didn't see why he shouldn't have normal toys, the same as any other kid. Mom looked a bit funny when she saw them.

"Look, Anna," she said, in the voice of one trying hard to be patient but finding it rather difficult, "you've got to accept facts. Benny's not like other babies. He's not going to be able to pile up those cups. He can't even pick things up and hold them properly. And it's no good wishing that he could."

I was really annoyed with Mom when she said that. Of course I knew Ben was different. What did she take me for? And what did she take Ben for, too? Even if he wasn't normal, he could learn to do some things. He might even get some fun out of it.

"I know, Mom." I said, in the voice of one trying hard to be polite but finding it rather difficult, "but I don't see why he can't just look at them and chew them a bit if he wants to."

I picked Ben up, and he snuggled his great big head down onto my shoulder. He couldn't talk or anything like that, but at long last he'd learned to kiss. I'd spent ages teaching him. You wouldn't believe that learning a little thing like kissing would be so difficult. It took nearly a week getting him to purse his lips, then another week to put them against my cheek, then two to make the actual kiss. One month of solid hard work. But when he did it for the first time, I felt so proud and happy it was like stars exploding inside my head. And Ben went mad with joy. He knew he'd been clever. He laughed and laughed and beat his weak little arms up and down in the air. Dr. Randall had been right about one thing, the night that Ben was born. Laughing was no problem. He could laugh all right.

Mind you, I had second thoughts about teaching Ben to kiss. I began to wish I'd taught him something else. The problem was that once he'd learned how to do it, he wouldn't stop. He never seemed to get bored with it. And no one else, except Mom, and sometimes Dad, seemed quite so eager to be kissed by Ben. Even I had to admit that his mouth was wetter than most people's.

"I think it's disgusting," Katy used to say, looking all prissy and stuck-up. "I don't know how you can stand it, getting dribbled all over like that."

A few weeks earlier I'd have pinched Katy good and hard for saying that, but I was growing too big for childish squabbles. Anyway, I'd realized that the poor child was suffering from the pangs of jealousy. They were no stranger to me. I knew how it felt to see one's best friend go off with a snotty little sycophant. That was one of my best descriptions of Emma. I'd thought up lots of them, especially just before going to sleep, but "snotty sycophant" combined, I thought, strict truthfulness and a neat elegance of phrasing. It was exquisitely crushing. I'd never dared say it to her face, but I was holding it in reserve. One day, I knew, my time for annihilating Emma would come.

I'd realized that Katy was jealous the day she shrieked at me, "You never play with me like you do with Ben. What do I have to do? Get myself handicapped or something?"

I was just about to tear her limb from limb when I suddenly understood, and a calm feeling of superiority came over me. I felt about fifty years old. So I smiled at her, and said very kindly, "Now, now, Katy, don't be jealous. Of course I'm really very fond of you."

But the wretched child just got madder than ever. After that I tried to ignore her. I promised myself that one day I'd do something really stunning for Katy, like taking her out for a hamburger or letting her listen to my golden oldie Beatles record. But I kept putting it off. The trouble was, she made me feel guilty. I really did like Ben much better than her. But did that mean I actually preferred him to be handicapped? That would be twisted and selfish. Still, when I thought about it, I decided it was okay. It was best to love Ben just for himself. Wishing couldn't make him any better, but loving him would make him happy. Perhaps that was what Mom had been trying to tell me.

Mom minded much more than I did about him being different. She avoided other babies. She never looked at them or tickled their tummies in the supermarket like she had done before Ben was born. I suppose she didn't want to think about what he might have been like. She just marched grimly on with him in his stroller, trying not to see the expressions on people's faces when they caught sight of him.

I didn't mind about the handicap as much as Mom, but I did mind about the way people looked at him. They'd see him, take one long, horrified stare, then their faces would kind of freeze up, and they'd gaze into the distance trying to pretend they hadn't noticed anything. But the minute your back was turned and you were hunting around the shelves for the cheapest jar of marmalade, you could practically feel their eyes boring into poor, innocent old Ben. He didn't care, mind you. He only went on holding his feet and trying to stuff them into his mouth, just like tiny babies do, only he was two years old.

I used to feel like a gladiator in ancient Rome girding himself up for battle before I went shopping with him. I used to avoid the main street, and walk on a bit farther, to the stores farthest away from the school. I'd never met anyone from school there, so I was lulled into a false sense of security. I used to put on his little coat, pull on his mittens, and get ready to stare down anyone who was rude. Actually, I had a worse time than Mom on these expeditions. People didn't dare say anything to her, but just because I looked younger than my age, more like an early thirteen than a middle fourteen, they took all kinds of liberties with me. Once a woman stopped me and said, "Do you mind, dear?" and got right down to really stare at Ben and then said, "What on earth's the matter with him? I've never seen one as bad as that before." She gave me a funny look, as if she thought I must be crazy or something.

I didn't mind children so much. They used to say what they thought right out loud, without trying to pretend. Things like, "Oh look, Mommy. That baby's got such a funny head." But I did mind the mothers who would look around and say, *"Shh,"* and pull the kids away. Why didn't they smile and say something nice? They could have said, "Yes, but he's got lovely curls," which was perfectly true. The worst time was when one horrible old woman with a beard muttered, "It's a shame letting a child like that out where a pregnant woman might see it. Oughtn't to be allowed."

I was so dumbstruck I couldn't think of a thing to say. I mean, what would you have done? But luckily I was at the newsstand, and Mrs. Chapman, who runs it, is a really nice person. She'd always been good about Ben.

"Silly old bat," she said. "Don't you take any notice

of her, Anna. Ben's lovely, aren't you, my duck?" and she leaned over her rack of Twixes and Mars bars so far that her great bosoms got tangled up in them, and she pulled a funny face at him. Ben went wild. He always laughed at Mrs. Chapman.

I loved her for that. Going to her shop and seeing her nice fat body squeeze between the shelves of sweets and newspapers and watching her wobble when she bent over Ben to give him a kiss made up for everyone else being funny about us.

"It's kids like this that teach us what loving's all about," she used to say. "You mark my words, Anna, they're special. I had a little cousin like this, you know. Ray of sunshine, she was."

In the end, though, it was Mrs. Chapman who led to my downfall. I'd gone shopping on Saturday morning and was in her store trying to choose a birthday card for Dad. Men are so difficult to buy things for, I find. One never knows what kind of thing they'll like. Ben was up near the counter, in his stroller, flapping his hands at Mrs. Chapman. I had rejected a joke card with a drunk trying to smoke forty cigarettes at once (it was Dad's fortieth birthday), because I didn't want to encourage him to take up bad habits at his time of life, and I was hesitating over an arty one of a lonely fisherman by a misty lake, when I heard a familiar voice.

"Oh, stop it, Greg. Oh, you are awful."

I froze. It was Miranda. She was the one in my class who was always twined around a boy. She had that kind of tight, bulgy body that seems about to burst out of its clothes, and she knew everything there was to know about sex. I tried not to listen when she got going in the coatroom. Call me a prig if you like, but I have my standards, and I draw the line at pornography. It degrades women.

My only hope was that Miranda and her horrible Greg would be so wrapped up in each other that they wouldn't notice me, or Ben. But I hadn't reckoned on Mrs. Chapman.

"Here, you two, mind the baby!" she called down the aisle, seeing them about to trip over the stroller. Miranda must have looked at Ben then, because I heard her say, "Oh my Gawd," in that silly way she does, and then giggle. I just hoped desperately that they wouldn't see me. I didn't even dare go on looking at the birthday cards. I bent my head right down and looked at the floor. To this day I could draw you a perfect sketch of the dusty floorboards, complete with all the cracks and knots in the wood. But I didn't get away with it. No such luck.

"Get Ben out of the way, Anna," Mrs. Chapman called to me, really loudly. "You don't want these lovebirds here to do him a mischief."

There was nothing else I could do then. I had to come out from behind the card stand. I felt my face flush flaming red and my hands go all wet with sweat. Miranda gasped when she saw me. If I hadn't been so upset, I'd have burst out laughing at her. She was so dressed up she looked ridiculous. I mean, down at the shops on a Saturday morning in our town isn't exactly the same as a Saturday night in Monte Carlo. And green spandex tights on one end of her and a plunging neckline at the other were too crude for words. But I was too flustered to think up anything witty that would give me the advantage. I wanted to turn tail and run.

"Is this Ben, your brother?" said Miranda, when she'd finally got her bright orange mouth working again.

"Yes, it is, actually," I said, "and if you've got any questions, comments, sick jokes, or wisecracks, now's your chance, Miranda."

She looked at me then, and I was sorry I'd been so hasty. She didn't look as if she wanted to laugh at all. She just shook her head a bit and said, "Knock it off, Pea-brain," in a quiet sort of voice, and trailed out of the shop, towing the deplorable Greg behind her.

I stood there trembling. I didn't know where I was for a moment. The floorboards heaved. Then I felt Mrs. Chapman's enormous soft arm around my shoulder.

"Hey," she said, "don't your school friends know about Ben, then?"

I shook my head.

"They didn't," I said, "but they will now."

Mrs. Chapman gave me a shake.

"Well," she said, "you may be a bit upset with me for letting the cat out of the bag, but I'm not going to say I'm sorry. You're a little idiot, Anna. You can't keep something like this a secret. It's high time your school friends knew about it. You're not ashamed of Benny, are you?"

"Course not," I said, but I knew I really was.

Mrs. Chapman did something she'd never done before. She took a Milky Way off the rack, tore off the paper, and gave it to me.

"It's on the house," she said. "First, last, and only

time. Now, come on, tell me. Why don't you want your friends to know? What are you so frightened of?"

It isn't easy having a really deep conversation with a newsdealer on a Saturday morning. People keep coming in to buy cigarettes, or to ask in husky voices for rude magazines from the top shelves, or to demand sympathy cards suitable for an old person whose goldfish has died. I vowed then and there never to become a shopkeeper. You have to have a butterfly mind. Mine is flighty enough without giving it any unnecessary encouragement.

Anyway, we managed all right. Mrs. Chapman got it all out of me, about how the girls at school didn't like me much and why I'd kept quiet about Ben because I didn't want to expose myself and I was afraid of being teased. Then she gave me a good talking to. The funny thing is, I didn't mind. She was so kind, and I knew she was talking sense. I trusted her. It was partly because she'd known and loved a handicapped child herself, but it was more than that. Mrs. Chapman was wise. She could look into the human heart and plumb its murky depths.

"What are you afraid of, then?" she said. "Sympathy? Don't be dumb, Anna. You can't have too much sympathy in this life. You need it. We all need it. But you've got to learn how to accept it. It's harder to be on the receiving end than the giving end sometimes. And you're not really afraid they'll laugh at you, are you? They're decent kids, deep down. Even that Marina, or Miranda, or whatever her name is, she's got a heart, you know. They'll only tease you if you're silly enough to go all proud and prickly, like you did just now, because then you're rejecting them. If you're honest and open and say, 'Look, it's true, my brother's severely handicapped and I never told you because I felt too miserable about it,' I bet you a bag of potato chips they'll be very nice about it.

"Why don't you tell them how you're trying to teach Ben things and show them how much he's learned? He can clap his hands now . . . can't you, my precious?" and she leaned down, wheezing a bit, and prodded Ben's tummy. He squirmed with pleasure. Then she straightened up again, putting one hand on her back to help herself.

"People are only scared of handicaps because they're not used to them," she went on. "You let them get to know Ben and see how you're so good at looking after him, and I bet they'll be all over him like bees round a honeypot, wanting to love him too."

Mrs. Chapman talked a long time, in between selling pencil sharpeners and candy bars, but she didn't quite convince me. I could just imagine the sly digs Emma would make and hear Debbie's cool, unconcerned voice saying rather grandly, "Well, you fooled us all, didn't you, Pee-wit? What made you think we'd be interested anyway?"

But Mrs. Chapman was right about one thing. The day after tomorrow I'd have to face them all at school. There was no getting away from that. And being frank and forthright was my only hope. There was no point in being stiff and starchy.

It was an awfully long wait until Monday.

Four

———

THERE'S A FUNNY THING I'VE NOTICED ABOUT LIFE. WHEN YOU really dread something, it turns out to be not so bad. It's the unexpectedly awful thing that gets you down.

Monday came at last. I'd worked myself up into such a state that Mom finally noticed. Dad hadn't been around much recently. He'd gotten a new job that kept him late at work, and even away at weekends sometimes. I missed him. I've always gotten along better with him than with Mom. She's so tactless. I mean, when I got a bit snappy over helping after supper, she ought to have realized I was upset and asked me nicely what the matter was. I was dying to tell her, actually. But instead she just said nastily, "I don't think I'll bother to cook you a nice supper in the future if you can't be bothered to help clear it up."

And Katy added her bit by ostentatiously getting the dishcloth and wiping the table. So, naturally, after that, I couldn't say a word.

On the day itself, I got to school early. I decided it would be best to get hold of Debbie on her own, before the whispers started spreading. Everyone listens to Debbie. If she decided to be nice, I wouldn't have anything to worry about. So I hung around the door to the coatroom, pretending to read the bit of *David Copperfield* we'd had for homework. That was a big mistake, because old Spenda came past and saw me.

"Do me a favor, Anna, will you?" she said. "Run over to the staff room and tell Mr. Henry there's a delivery of books waiting for him in the office. Mrs. Clark wants them out of her way."

It was a disaster. There was nothing I could do. I mumbled something that would have been much ruder if I hadn't liked old Spenda so much and tore off at top speed to get there and back as soon as possible. Just past the gym, I ran into Vicky.

"Do me a favor, will you, Vick?" I said. "Can you take this message to Mr. . . ."

"No," said Vicky, transferring a disgusting blob of gum from one cheek to the other and looking wide-eyed at me with that maddening grin she puts on when she wants to see how much she can irritate you. No wonder she's a social outcast. I've done my best for Vicky, like giving her a Christmas card last year and sitting beside her at lunch on Thursdays during Lent, but some people don't want you to be nice to them.

By the time I'd found Mr. Henry and bolted back to the coatroom, I'd been reprimanded by two teachers for running in the corridor and I'd lost my chance of getting Debbie alone. I could see her smooth chestnut hair sticking up several inches above a knot of black, brown, and blond heads, and I could tell even from a distance that they were all listening, with riveted attention, to Miranda.

"I've never seen anything like it," she said. "I mean, this great big head, like a monster in a weird cartoon."

Something clicked inside me. I dropped my bag and raced over to the group. They stepped back when they saw me coming. Every face was agog with curiosity, and not one displayed even a drop of the milk of human kindness. Perhaps that was why I was suddenly possessed by a magnificent anger, held in check by superhuman force, and the strength of an iron calm.

"My brother Benedict," I said to Miranda, "is not a monster, and if I ever hear you, or anyone else in this room, using that word again, I will personally murder you with my bare hands."

There was a total, unnatural silence. The entire coatroom, full of about thirty girls, was listening.

"But," I went on, "he is severely handicapped. He's got hydrocephalus. He'll never be like other children, but he knows how to laugh and love people, and he's sweet, and adorable, and if you want to know why I didn't tell you before, it's because I knew you'd call him dreadful things and laugh at him, and he's not a . . . not a . . ." and then I burst into tears.

Looking back, I suppose it was the best thing I could have done, though I felt like an awful fool at the time. But I couldn't have kept up the magnificent anger, and so forth, for much longer. They all flocked around me, anyway, and I heard Miranda say, "Honestly, I didn't mean . . ." and Debbie, sounding uncharacteristically furious, saying, "Shut up, you. You've done enough already." And then she thrust a tissue into my hand and said, "Poor old Pee-wit, you should have told us ages ago. We're really sorry about it. You can see that, can't you?"

And then the bell rang for the first lesson.

The news about Ben spread around the school like wildfire. I knew it would. But I had no idea everyone would be so nice about it. People kept coming up to me and saying things like, "God, how awful," and "Poor old Pea-brain," and offering me bits of chocolate. I usually try not to eat chocolate because of my skin, but I saw each piece as an olive branch and felt it my duty to accept. Even Emma lent me her pencil sharpener. It was the first time she'd ever been civil. Miranda grabbed me as soon as the bell rang for break.

"Anna, please," she said. "I've been feeling so bad. I didn't mean to be horrible. Honestly, I'm really sorry, but you were so . . ."

"I know, I was rude in the shop," I said. "It was my fault as much as yours." I felt magnanimous toward everyone, even Miranda. The truth was that I felt as if a great burden had rolled off my shoulders. I actually bounced when I walked because I felt physically lighter. It was such a relief, such a blissful, wonderful relief to be rid of the secret of Ben, and to find that people seemed to like me more, not less.

When I was on my way to the playground, Mrs. Gordon called me into her study. She's the vice principal and thinks a lot about dignity. I've never felt the same about her since I saw her through a crack in the staff-room door stubbing out a cigarette and putting a peppermint into her mouth to take the smell away. It's not that I disapprove of smokers. I know there are people who are victims to a helpless addiction too strong for them to break. But Minnie Gordon had just given us a lecture on health and told us never to touch tobacco. I'm pretty sure she actually denied smoking herself, though I wouldn't swear to it. Old hypocrite. Today, however, she was quite affable, for her.

"Ah, there you are, Anna," she said. "I'm sorry to hear about your brother. It must be very hard for your mother."

There's the typical adult reaction for you. They think that parents are the only ones who are capable of feeling things. They don't realize that it's not exactly easy for brothers and sisters, either.

"You should have told me a long time go," she said. "The school needs to be informed about problems at home." And she swept past me and on to some pressing duty, pleased with herself for being so compassionate. But I noticed that her back view was a mess. Her hem was coming down and she had a run in her stockings.

You've got a problem at home, I thought. Secret drinking, I shouldn't wonder.

After that it was just another day—until English in the afternoon. Spenda was making us read poems out loud. They were all about animals. I don't know whether she was being terribly clever and subtle, or whether it was just by accident, but she seemed to choose exactly the right person to read each poem. Debbie did one about an eagle, living "Close to the sun in azure lands." Emma read the one about the snake, "writhing like lightning." Very appropriate. The next poem was called "The Donkey." Spenda looked around the class.

"Your turn, I think, Anna." She smiled nicely, though.

I like reading poetry aloud. I put in lots of expression and pause dramatically in the right places. Verse one was fine. But as my eye ran on to verse two, the words jumped off the page at me.

With monstrous head and sickening cry
And ears like errant wings . . .

I stood there, dumb as a donkey myself. I couldn't read a word of it.

"Go on, Anna," said Spenda. "What's wrong with you?"

"With monstrous head . . ." I began, seeing there was nothing I could do about it, and then I caught Debbie's eye. She had her hand over her mouth, and her eyes were dancing, and she was trying desperately not to burst out laughing. Of course, I caught it from her and started to giggle, and the whole class began to shriek, and we laughed and laughed, with poor old Spenda looking around us all and saying helplessly, "What on earth's the matter with you all? What's it all about? Will you please stop it, at once!"

That only made us worse, of course. We'd try to stop, but then someone would give a wail of laughter, and we'd all start up again, but eventually she managed to shut us up, and except for the odd gasp and hiccup, we got through to the end of the lesson. I'll say one thing for Spenda. She didn't go all huffy and try to make us explain. Goodness knows what we'd have said. She didn't even make us finish reading the poem. She got us going on cruelty to animals instead. It was really interesting.

I felt wonderful after that lesson. The tension had all been laughed away. They'd been laughing with me, not at me. I was one of the crowd again.

In gym I plucked up my courage and asked Debbie if she'd like to come home with me after school. I didn't think she'd accept, but she jumped at it. I suspected it was mostly vulgar curiosity, but I didn't blame her. It couldn't hurt Ben, after all. He had no idea what embarrassment was. He'd never been offended in his life.

The surprising thing, though, was Mom's reaction. She looked amazed when she saw Debbie. It's a dreadful thing to admit, but when we came into the kitchen and I saw her slopping about in her dirty old slippers, with her hair half frizzled and half straight from the perm that was still growing out, I felt ashamed. I saw her through Debbie's eyes and suddenly realized how much she'd changed over the past two years. I suppose she'd been so tied to the house with Ben and everything that she'd stopped bothering about herself. It had been ages since she'd bought herself something new, or even put on any makeup.

"Where's Ben?" I said.

I saw her eyes open with alarm.

"He's asleep," she said, "You can't . . ." but at that moment I heard him crowing. There must have been a pigeon on his windowsill, because that always made him laugh. I put bread out especially to attract them. If one was pecking away when Ben woke up, he'd open his eyes and start laughing right off. It was the happiest noise you could imagine.

I couldn't wait to get Debbie out of the kitchen before she could notice the stains on Mom's apron or the hole in her tights. I pushed her out the door and up the stairs, my heart hammering.

Ben was in his crib. He had learned to sit up by himself, and I was trying to teach him to reach up for the top rail and pull himself up to a standing position. He hadn't gotten there yet, but we were working on it. When he saw me, he did what he always did, reached out his arms and roared with joy. I lifted him up and danced around the room with him. I was putting off the moment when I'd have to look at Debbie.

When I did, I couldn't see her face. She was bending over her bag, and then she straightened up with a chocolate bar in her hand.

"Is he allowed to eat it?" she asked.

"Oh, he loves chockies, yummy yummy chockies, don't you, my little Benny-Ben?" I said. I knew I sounded silly, but I couldn't stop prattling. I was too nervous. But then I shot a look at Debbie and shut up. She was gazing at Ben with a really concentrated expression. It wasn't nasty prying, it was interested, even kindly.

"Does it hurt?" she said. "His head must be difficult to hold up, it's so big and such a funny shape."

"No, it doesn't seem to hurt," I said. I'd sort of calmed down because she was being so matter-of-fact.

"It's awful when he gets a cold, though. He really has to fight for breath. Mom's been up with him all through the night."

"She must be exhausted," said Debbie. "I'm a wreck if I don't get my eight hours. I don't know how she does it."

"She's got to do it. She doesn't have much choice," I said. Actually, I hadn't really thought about it before. Mom had been getting up in the night for so long that I'd gotten used to it. I'd stopped asking myself how she managed. I just took it for granted.

Debbie's mind is so transparent that you can practically see the cogs going around. That's the good thing about her. She's incapable of being deceitful. She can be infuriating and mean and cutting and fickle, but you'll always know where you are with her. She's sort of detached from life, as if she were peering at other mortals through a microscope or from outer space or something. It gets her into awful trouble. I'll never forget the time Mrs. Gordon lost her temper because Debbie had let a door swing shut in Mrs. G's face, and Debbie said, "Sorry," in such a cool, unconcerned voice that Mrs. G went raging mad. Debbie just stood there watching her with a kind of scientific interest. When Mrs. G stopped to draw breath and stick a few hairpins back into her scraggy gray chignon, Debbie said, as cool as a cucumber, "Excuse my saying so, Mrs. Gordon, but I think you ought to see the dentist. You've got bad breath."

Mrs. Gordon stood there for a moment, as one turned to stone, then shut her mouth with a snap and marched off to report Debbie to the principal, but nothing ever came of it. Emma said the principal probably fainted at the stench of Mrs. G's breath, and told her she was an undesirable alien. The funny thing was, though, that Debbie was really surprised about all the fuss. She said she'd only been giving Mrs. G some well-meant advice and she should have been grateful.

So I wasn't surprised when Debbie asked a lot of impertinent questions about Ben. I didn't mind a bit. Then I said, "Would you like to hold him?"

Her scientific detachment deserted her all of a sudden, and she looked a bit nervous, blinking those big, beautiful brown eyes of hers and shaking her sleek brown hair out of them. She stepped back.

"I might hurt him, or drop him or something," she said. "I don't know about babies."

"Don't be a fool," I said, and plopped him straight into her arms.

She held him stiffly for a minute, then tried to turn him around. Once she'd done it and Ben was directly opposite her face, the result was inevitable. He pushed out his lips and kissed her cheek. Unfortunately, I'd already given him a piece of chocolate bar, and some sticky brown dribble was running down his chin.

Debbie is one of the most fastidious people I know. She gets up at dawn every day to wash her hair, and she told me when she stopped being my best friend that though she liked my personality, she couldn't face my pimples, buck teeth, and greasy hair. They offended her aesthetic sensibilities. It hurt terribly at the time, but I know she didn't mean to be unkind. It was just the sort of horribly frank and honest thing that Debbie was always saying. She thought she was giving me a perfectly reasonable explanation.

I stood waiting for her to look disgusted and thrust Ben back at me. But instead she looked startled.

"He kissed me!" she said. "Or was it an accident?"

"No, I taught him to kiss," I said. "It took ages. I'd no idea there was so much skill in it."

"But that's amazing," said Debbie, wiping her cheek. "I thought he'd be a kind of living lump, just eating and breathing. Do you mean he can actually learn things and make friends with people, like an ordinary person?"

If anyone else had said that, I'd have thumped them. Living lump indeed! But you have to keep reminding yourself that Debbie's a special case. She's socially primitive. She only gets away with it because she's so beautiful.

"Of course he can learn things," I said. "I've taught him to clap his hands. Watch this."

She put Ben down on the floor, and he performed perfectly.

"What else can he do?" said Debbie.

"I'm trying to teach him to stand up," I said. "Look."

I pushed my fingers into Ben's closed fists. He grasped them, and I pulled him up onto his feet. He stood there for a moment, frowning earnestly, then plumped down onto his bottom again and laughed. You could see he was pleased with himself.

Debbie was quite enthusiastic.

"You could teach him all sorts of things," she said.

"He might even catch up if you worked hard enough. You could teach him to talk." She picked up Ben's hand and pointed at it.

"Hand," she said very loudly. "Say 'hand.'"

"You can't do that," I said. "It'll be years before he learns to say anything. And he might not, even then. There's no point in ever thinking he'll be the same as other kids. He just won't. You've got to be realistic and start from where he's at. Even learning the simplest things, like putting a chocolate bar in his mouth, are like climbing Mount Everest to him."

Ben had curled his fingers around one of Debbie's and was staring at it. You could see he was concentrating hard. Debbie must have liked the feel of it, because she said, "I think he's cute. Sort of different and special. I wish you'd told me about him before, Anna. I'd like to have seen him when he was tiny. It must be fun teaching him things. Can I come back and see him again?"

"Yes," I said, "oh yes, any time you like, Debbie, any time at all."

She picked up her bag and slung it over her shoulder with the kind of easy grace I'll never learn even if I live to be a hundred and three and do yoga exercises every day.

"Good-bye," she said. "See you tomorrow."

"I thought you'd stay for tea," I said, trying not to look disappointed.

"Can't," she said. "I've got choir practice tonight."

I went downstairs with her and saw her out. Then I shut the front door and turned to see Mom behind me.

She'd changed and done her hair and put some makeup on.

"I thought Debbie was staying for tea," she said.

"No, she's got choir tonight," I said.

Mom looked uncertain. I knew what she wanted to ask, and I knew she wouldn't be able to.

"I told them at school about Ben today," I said, putting her out of her misery. "Miranda saw me last week with him, and it was all around the class. I thought they'd be awful, but they were really nice. I wish I'd told everyone years ago. And Mom, Debbie likes him. She really does. She thinks he's special, and she'd like to come again."

I didn't wait for that sort of remote look that comes over Mom's face whenever I mention Debbie. She thinks Debbie's a little madam and gets away with murder and needs her bottom spanked. Mom doesn't understand that beauty and charm exact their toll. I was so pleased that I ran down the hall and took a running jump at the light. I used to do that a lot when I was a kid, but it's not the sort of thing you do much when you're fourteen. I hadn't reckoned on the fact that I'd grown, so instead of just tipping the shade a bit with my fingers, I gave it a proper whack by mistake, and it swung about wildly. I thought Mom would be irritated, but she laughed.

"You look happy today," she said. "It was lovely seeing you coming in with a friend, like you used to. It's been a long time."

"Yes," I said, "and it's lovely seeing you look so nice and pretty, with lipstick and everything. That's been a long time too."

"I didn't want to let you down in front of Debbie," she said. "Give me a bit more warning next time."

We stood there, like a pair of idiots, smiling at each other. Then Mom said, "Come on, let's have a cup of tea," and I said, "Why not?" and we settled down at the kitchen table like a couple of real grown-up friends having a chat. I'd never felt sort of equal with Mom before, like I was a woman and understood her problems, but I did that afternoon. We didn't say much, just little things, like how Ben was getting on learning to stand and how awful it was Dad never being around on weekends, and I said why didn't Mom leave Ben with me on Saturday; and go down to the shops and buy herself something nice to wear, and Mom said why didn't she make me an appointment at the new salon on Main Street to have my hair cut, and then she suddenly looked at the clock and said,

"Oh Lord, I've got to pick Katy up from Tracey's party."

I laughed, and said, "Bet she insisted on wearing her party shoes to school today," and Mom laughed, too, and said,

"You know what she's like." Then she went, and I did the washing up without her asking me and set the table for supper and settled Ben down in front of the TV because there was a pop music show on, and he loved listening to music. And I felt about twenty-five years old, and mature, and grown up, and wise.

Five

———

THE SUMMER THAT BEN WAS TWO IS BATHED IN A ROSY SORT OF sunset in my memory. I can't believe I was so carelessly happy, or that I didn't have a premonition of what was going to happen. It was one of those long, hot summers when the days seem to go on forever and everyone is lazy and languorous and people stop bothering to make you clean your room and it's fatally easy to fall in love.

It didn't start off well, though. We were all depressed because we couldn't go away for a vacation. Katy pestered Mom and Dad on and on for a week about the Costa del Sol. Her friend Tracey had gone there, so Katy thought it was the last word in cosmopolitan sophistication. I wouldn't have minded a vacation there myself, I must say, but I knew better than to nag. I finally dragged Katy off into my bedroom and gave her a proper talking to.

"Will you shut up about vacations?" I said. "Can you imagine us on an airplane with Ben? How do you think it would feel pushing him up and down the promenade in Benidorm? Do you like the idea of feeding him his breakfast in a crowded hotel dining room?"

Comprehension dawned. I'll say one thing for Katy, she's not slow. Then she scowled, and kicked my bed. She did it harder than she meant to and hurt her toe and had to hop around the room holding on to her foot.

"Ben!" she said, when she was finally capable of saying anything. "It's always Ben! Mom won't take me swimming because she can't leave Ben. I couldn't have a proper birthday party like Tracey's because Mom's so tired looking after Ben. Now we can't even go away on vacation like a normal, ordinary family. I sometimes wish . . ."

"What do you sometimes wish, miss?" I said, my voice dangerously quiet and menacing. Katy knew I'd scalp her if she wasn't careful, so she just said sulkily, "Oh nothing."

"I suppose you think we should put Ben in some horrid home, with cruel nurses, while we go off and have a good time?" I said, with awful sarcasm. She pouted.

"I suppose you wouldn't care if he got one of his colds and there was no one there he knew to pick him up in the night and comfort him," I went on, remorselessly.

Katy suddenly jumped up and turned on me.

"Of course I would," she said. "Don't be such a pig! I don't want him to be miserable." And she darted out of my room, and I heard her crashing down the stairs and out into the garden, where Ben was sitting as good as gold in his playpen, studying a leaf that had fallen into it. And she danced around him singing, "We all live in a yellow submarine," in her high-pitched, tuneless voice while Ben clapped his hands and shrieked as he always did. That's another good thing about Katy, I must admit. Underneath her irritating exterior she's got a kind little heart. She'll stick by you if you're really in trouble. It's just that you have to be really in trouble first.

Mind you, I'm not saying that I didn't care about the vacation. Of course I did. When I was little, we used to rent a cottage in the country for two weeks in August, a different one every year. There was no thrill like the excitement of following the written instructions, and arriving, and piling out of the car, and exploring the whole place, and deciding who would sleep in which bedroom. Each cottage had something especially nice about it. One, I remember, had an old apple tree in the back garden that you could climb. I spent whole afternoons up there, with a cushion, an apple, and a book. Another had a field beside it with ponies in it, and I used to go and feed them handfuls of grass every morning and whisper things into their soft, flickering ears, which smelled deliciously of horse. But there was no point in wishing. I knew quite well that we had to stay at home.

Dad knew it was tough for us, seeing our friends go away. I overheard him and Mom talking about it one night. I didn't mean to snoop, but they were in the garden, and I was in my bedroom, with the window open, and it was one of those still summer nights when sound carries further than usual.

"Katy was very grumpy at bedtime tonight," said Mom. "I can't think what gets into that child sometimes."

"She had a postcard from Tracey this morning, from Spain," said Dad. "Poor thing's feeling left out."

That was typical of Mom and Dad. She couldn't work out what the matter was, but Dad seemed to just know. There was a silence, then Mom gave a big sigh.

"I suppose we couldn't, could we?" she said, a little uncertainly.

"Of course we couldn't," said Dad, in his crisp I-am-the-manager-of-this-firm voice. "And if anyone needs a holiday, it's you. The girls will just have to take second place at the moment. Look, we could get a nurse in for a few nights, and I'd manage in the day. I could take a week off. They owe me that at least after all I've been doing for the last six months. And you could go off for a week with Janice or your mother."

"No!" said Mom, and her voice sounded sort of cracked. "I couldn't leave him! Every time it gets worse. Oh, Peter, if only you'd been here when he had that cold last month. It was no more than a chill, and honestly he was fighting for his life. I don't know how I'll bear it . . ." And then I heard her crying, and Dad moving his chair, and then muffled noises, so I shut the window because, although I couldn't help listening to them talking, I didn't want to hear them kissing and everything. It turns me off when old people do it.

They must have talked some more, because the next morning, at breakfast, Dad still had on his bright, breezy, organizing manner that he gets sometimes, when he decides that things have become too slack at home and it needs a man to put them right. He'd been out shopping before breakfast and had come back with croissants and the local paper. He took Mom's breakfast up to her on a tray. Ben had been awake a lot in the night, he said, and she needed to sleep in. Then he unfolded the paper and made a great show of finding the "Summer Events for Children" column.

"Ah!" he said at last, and pushed his glasses down to the tip of his nose so that he could pretend to look intellectual.

"Swimming. Daily courses in lifesaving and diving. Ages five to eleven."

"It's booked up, Daddy. Mom phoned last week," Katy said. She was in a bad mood and would have turned down tea at Buckingham Palace if she'd been invited.

"Riding," Dad read out. Katy's eyes brightened. She looked interested in spite of herself. Dad looked down the ad and saw the prices.

"On second thought, bad idea," he said. "Riding develops the bottom. Turns to fat in middle age," and he went on hastily to the next item.

"Outward Bound."

I gave him a look.

"Dad . . ." I said. He looked up at me and smiled.

"Okay, okay," he said. "Say no more."

An ad on the opposite page caught his eye.

"Wedding dress, size twelve, unused, only fifty dollars. Mmm, they must have quarreled at the last minute. I wonder if they're trying to sell the cake as well?"

I could see his mind had wandered and it would take a week to get it back on course again, so I tweaked the paper out of his hand.

"Here, do you mind?" he said. But I had found what I was looking for.

"Tennis course, two hours daily, professional coaches, places still available."

"There you are," I said triumphantly. "That's what I want to do."

I didn't dare tell anyone, but I'd been nursing a secret ambition. It was partly because I'd been watching Wimbledon all through June, but it was also the result of a freak streak of brilliance I'd suddenly developed in the last week of the summer term. I had astonished myself with a series of ace serves and a spate of shots that made even Debbie gasp. In the very last lesson before the vacation I was playing doubles with Miranda against Miss Winter and Sandra. I suddenly astounded everyone by foreseeing the exact angle at which Miss Winter's wicked top spin whizzed over the net and ricocheted off the tarmac, and then by positioning myself exactly right and whacking it back with such precision that it skimmed the net and flew between Sandra's legs before she had time to jump. So sweet had been the praises that had fallen from everyone's lips (I had grown out of my hopeless passion for Miss Winter but retained a kind of loyalty to the sacred memory of love), and so delightful the shoulder clappings I received as I modestly retired from the court, that I had decided to work my game up into something really sensational and spring it on an astonished world next summer.

Dad was delighted. He had solved the problem of how I would spend my time. Now he only had to deal with Katy. I could see he was already congratulating himself on being so well organized and resourceful.

He had underestimated Katy. Half an hour later she had driven us both to screaming point. She had turned down a drama workshop, ballet lessons, a sports week, trampolining, and junior watersports. She had refused to go and stay with Granny, Aunty Janice, and the Watsons, who used to be our next-door neighbors but moved a year ago. She had insisted that, since she couldn't go to Benidorm like Tracey, she would spend every day at home, sulking, and too bad if we didn't like it. She had entirely forgotten our little talk of the day before. That's the trouble with children. They can't stick to anything. Once they get an idea in their heads, they bring it up again and again, and there's no point your thinking that you've knocked it out, because you haven't.

"All right," said Dad at last. "I give up. It's tennis lessons for one, sulks for the other. Katy can make herself useful at home minding Ben."

Katy could not stop herself looking anxious.

"I'll go and telephone the tennis place now," said Dad, "and fix it all up for you, Spanner." He spent a long time putting the newspaper together again. I could see he was giving Katy a last chance to change her mind. She fell for it.

"Well, I suppose, if I've got to, I could do tennis too," she said at last. I sighed. Typical. She would want to do the same as me. Now I'd have her trailing after me every day, cramping my style, nosing into everyone I spoke to and being a general nuisance. I was so irritated I slammed the door as I went out, not quite loud enough to get reprimanded for, but enough to make my feelings plain to everyone sensitive enough to read the signs. I knew it would do no good to protest. I was stuck with Katy, and I might as well accept it.

Actually, when I'd calmed down, it didn't seem such a bad idea. I realized that she could be quite useful. It probably wouldn't be easy to get enough people to practice with. If Katy only learned to get the ball over the net, I could practice smashing them back. And she'd never complain. It would be better than nobody anyway. Not much better, but still better. I decided to go downstairs quickly again, and pretend that it had been the wind that had slammed the door and see if Dad would give me some money for new sneakers and a racket. He might even be so relieved and pleased with himself for sorting out our summer vacation that he'd pay for one of those pretty tennis outfits like the stars at Wimbledon wear. It was worth a try anyway.

So that was how it all began, that happy, carefree summer, the last of my untrammeled youth.

If I'm going to be absolutely honest, I must admit that it wasn't only the tennis that was luring me down to the courts. It was Ted's Snackbar too. The tennis courts were in a corner of the Recreation Ground, which was just a field with some trees around the edge and a playground with things like swings and sandpits. Between the swings and the courts was this kind of open-air café. It was only a hut, really, where old Ted sold coffee and tea and ices, but you could watch any games going on on the courts, and mess around on the swings if the park keeper wasn't there (they were supposed to be out of bounds for the over-fourteens). Old Ted didn't take any notice of what anyone did. He just read his newspaper all day and only popped his head out when there was somebody waiting to put some money into his grubby old till. Anyway, that was where the scene was that summer. Miranda had practically lived there since the end of the term. She was always shrieking around and showing off, and then disappearing behind a tree with one of the boys.

I didn't want to be like Miranda, exactly, but I did want to see what was going on. I wanted to sort of try myself out a bit. Since that day when Debbie had come home with me, my life had really changed. Mom had started to notice me for the first time in years. She seemed to realize that I was now more than ten years old. She'd even gotten to work on my looks. She'd bought me contact lenses and made me go to an expensive hairdresser, who had given me a different kind of shampoo so that my hair wasn't quite so greasy. I still had pimples, but they were getting better, only a couple at a time, and sometimes none at all. Dare I say it, I looked quite good sometimes. Even Debbie noticed a change in me.

"It's not that you're pretty, exactly," she said, wrinkling up her perfect nose while I waited anxiously for the verdict, "though you've got a touch of style now, I must say. It's more . . . it's like there's a kind of electricity in you that gives off a flash from time to time, and then you kind of radiate. It's cool."

Emma hated it when Debbie took any notice of me, and she'd put her word in at once.

"We'd better keep out of your way, then," she said, giggling in that awful moronic way of hers, "or we'll get contaminated with the fallout when you have one of your c-o-o-l flashes."

Debbie hadn't laughed, but she hadn't stopped Emma from dragging her away either. I think she was too lazy to resist Emma's iron will.

Nothing much happened the first few afternoons down at the Rec. There weren't many people about, and Miranda didn't come at all. But on Thursday afternoon the place was suddenly crowded. As luck would have it, I was looking really good. Dad had been generous about the tennis stuff. I had these great sneakers and a really nice dress. I'd pointed out to him that he was saving himself a fortune by not taking us all to Costa del Sol, and he'd taken the hint. I was wearing my lenses too. I'd gotten to the point where I could keep them in for about four hours without wanting to scratch my eyes out.

At the end of every lesson, Terry (the coach) and I used to play a few real games, and I was in the middle of my serve when I saw Miranda and the gang coming. I did a double take. I was suddenly terrified in case any under-arm hair was popping out of my short sleeve when I lifted up my arm, so I twisted myself around to serve, so that they'd only see the back of my shoulder, and nearly ruptured myself bringing the racket down on the ball at a funny angle. There was a sort of grunt, and a squeak of amazement from Terry, because by some incredible chance it had turned into a smashing ace, and he'd had to duck to avoid being assassinated.

"Brilliant, Anna!" he boomed, scratching his hairy

chest in the gap where his button-up T-shirt was gaping open. Terry had some revolting personal habits, but he was a fantastic coach. He made good tennis come as easily as eating bread and honey.

I saw Miranda's head swivel around when she heard my name, and I could see her sort of squinting at me against the sun, through her great mop of hair, trying to decide if it was me or not. Then Katy, who was kicking herself around on one of those playground carousel things while she was waiting for me to finish with Terry, called out, "Hello, Miranda?" and Miranda recognized her and realized it must be me.

Miranda may be boy-crazy, but she's not the kind who won't have anything to do with other girls. She's got a friendly nature. That's her problem, Mom always says. Too friendly. Anyway, she shook off the boy who'd got his arm draped around her neck and came to shout encouragement to me through the wire fence. I saw she was carrying a racket.

"Are you going to play?" I said.

"Yeah," she said. "We're doing doubles."

"Who's 'we'?" I asked.

"Oh, me and Joe against Barny and Tony."

I didn't have time for any more, because Terry was working on my backhand, and he kept shoving one awful ball at me after the other, but I saw them out of the corner of my eye as they went into the next court. I knew Joe and Barny vaguely. I'd seen them at the youth center I used to go to ages ago. I didn't recognize the other one. But funnily enough, even though I only saw him out of the corner of my eye, I was aware of him at once. He had that kind of pantherish walk, sort of elegant but full of suppressed power that you felt might break out at any minute.

Then Terry and I changed sides because the sun was right in his eyes, and he said that at my age I could stand it better than him, so I walked around the net on the side nearest Miranda's court and got a closer look.

I've noticed something really interesting about first impressions. When I see someone for the first time, before I've even talked to them or anything, I get a kind of instant glimpse of what they're really like. Then, when I get to know them a bit, the picture changes and they seem quite different. But once I get to know them really well, I often find that the very first impression was nearer the truth than the second one.

That's how it was with Tony. I can see him now as I first saw him, just as if I had a photograph of him in my head. He was standing a bit apart from the other three and listening to them, not smiling, but looking rather remote. His dark hair fell in a heavy shock over his forehead, and his eyes were brilliant and direct, with long, dark lashes that made them look even bigger. His mouth had a kind of twist to it which could have been mocking or unhappy. I could see that Miranda was smitten. She kept wriggling out of Joe's reach, though she'd been happily making a spectacle of herself with him all over town since the end of last term, and edging up toward Tony. He kept moving away, not nastily, but in an almost too polite kind of way that made him seem dignified and untouchable, and above all that sort of thing. But I could see, in that first, brilliant snapshot, that he wasn't at all cold and withdrawn the way he seemed. I could sense someone else in him, someone intense, and lonely, and locked up. It sounds corny, I know, but so what? The corniest things are usually the truest, I think, anyway.

Their game started. Mine was nearly over. They weren't very good. At least Tony wasn't bad. He had a natural kind of speed and grace, but he didn't seem to have played tennis much. Once, while he was waiting for Barny to take Joe's serve, I saw that he was watching me, and I'd just done a particularly showy save from the net. Then Terry started one of his firework volleys that sent the ball over again and again as fast as a meteor shower. When I finally missed the last one, it crashed into the wire fence that separated the two courts, and I crashed after it, because I'd been running so fast to get it, and as luck would have it, at exactly the same moment Tony was retrieving a ball from the same spot on the other side. We were suddenly only a couple of inches away from each other. I think I must have given off one of my electric flashes, because I saw a tiny answering spark in his brown eyes, then he dropped his eyelids and said, "Sorry." I can't think why, because we hadn't actually bumped into each other or anything, and then he strolled back to his game.

That was all it was, that first meeting. But it was enough to pierce my lousy defenses, which, when it came to love, were absolutely useless. And I kept telling myself I was being a huge, number-one prize-winning twit. Tony was by far the most attractive boy I'd ever seen. And with all the Mirandas of this world trailing after him, I would never have a chance with him.

Usually, after I'd finished with Terry, Katy and I had an ice cream at Ted's, and then we went home, but that day I was desperate to stick around. I pretended to be listening to Terry's little lecture, the one he always gives at the end of a coaching session, when all the time I was trying to think of a good excuse for not going home. In the end I needn't have bothered. Good old Katy came to my rescue. She walked up to the netting, bold as brass, and called out, "Miranda! Hey, Miranda! Do you want me to ball-boy?"

Of course Miranda said yes. Then, as an after-thought, Katy said, "You don't mind, do you, Annie?" and I said, as casually as I could, "No, that's okay," and then I got a Coke from Ted and sat down on the swing, with my right side facing the courts because my hair's parted on the left so my right profile is the better one.

I must have sat there for half an hour at least. Usually I can't bear just sitting around with nothing to do. I can't even bear to go to the bathroom if I don't have something to read in there. In fact, I've had several near misses hunting for a book to take in with me. Mad, really. But that day I could have sat there forever.

It was partly the sun filtering through the trees and making the boring old Rec look mellow and dignified, like a park around a stately home (except that the back end of the Colliston Road flats couldn't possibly be mistaken for a stately home), and partly the hypnotic effect of the swing, which had a rhythmic sort of singsong squeak and lifted my hair in a lovely warm breeze every time I went forward. But of course, it was mainly being near Tony and wondering what would happen when the game was over.

My lovely daydream of being a kind of countess or something and having tea under the big elm on the south lawn from a tray that the butler had set up on a white Italian-style table was rudely shattered when Katy suddenly yelled, "Mom!" and dashed out of the court and raced off over the grass to where Mom had appeared, pushing Ben in the stroller.

I stopped swinging then. I hadn't bargained for Ben that afternoon. Barny and Joe were all right. I didn't care about them. And Miranda had seen Ben lots of times. I'd even taken him to school one day. Spenda had gotten us to do a project on the handicapped, and Ben had come along to meet the class. He'd been a sensation. In fact, dear old Ben had become a kind of mascot. The numbers of useless jackets the girls had knitted for him, you wouldn't believe. But it was Tony I was wondering about. I couldn't guess what his reaction would be.

They finished their game and came out of the court just as Mom arrived at the swings. Ben was wriggling about fretfully.

"He saw a little girl over there with an ice cream," said Mom. "Can you get him one, Anna?"

She gave me some money, and I went over to Ted's. By the time he'd put his paper down and fished around in his freezer and dug out Ben's favorite ice-pop, poor old Ben was crying properly. I peeled the paper off and gave it to him, then looked around for Tony. He'd gone. All I could see was his back as he ran lightly down the path onto the main road toward the bus stop.

Six

It WAS ODD GOING BACK TO SCHOOL AFTER THE SUMMER. THEY'D switched all the classes around. I'd been with Debbie and Sandra and Vicky and Miranda and all the rest of them ever since I was eleven, and all of a sudden there were a lot of different faces. I felt quite lost for a week or two. I mean, if you've spent half your waking life with the same bunch of people for years and years, you get sort of dependent on them, whether you really like them or not, and when half of them aren't there anymore, you feel strange. It's like moving or something.

Debbie and Emma were still in my class, and so was Miranda. They were taking arts subjects like me. But Vicky and Gloria, as well as Sandra and all her clever friends, had gone into the science class. I'd never hung around with them much. They were too high-powered. But they were better than the load of silly gigglers we got instead. Karen and Bella were the worst. I couldn't help despising them. I know you shouldn't be an intellectual snob, but they seemed to have gotten stuck at the mental age of nine. They were awful in English lessons.

They couldn't take literature seriously. I'd become quite enthusiastic about it, actually. I used to read Keats in bed and learn chunks by heart. I thought it was so awful the way he died so young and everything. I tried writing some poems myself sometimes and left them on my desk, hoping that Mom would read them and tell me they were brilliant. But she just tidied everything into a heap when she did my room and never seemed to notice. Just like her.

We had a new English teacher, Mrs. Hamilton. She had white hair, but she had it cut fashionably, as if she was still only eighteen or something. It looked clever and sort of timeless. I wished my Mom would be a bit less boring about her clothes and everything. When I'm forty, I'm going to stay in tune with youth. I'm going to remember exactly what it's like to be fifteen, and I'm going to have a deep and special sympathy with unattractive girls. And that's a promise.

Mrs. Hamilton wasn't just interesting to look at. She did odd things too. She used to stride up and down, throwing out her hands in striking gestures so that her gold bangles clunked together. But the minute there was anything the slightest bit sexy, Karen would start sniggering and set Bella off.

Mrs. Hamilton bore it for a week or two, and then she struck. We were doing poets of the seventeenth century, and she was reading Andrew Marvell.

An hundred years should go to praise
Thine eyes and on thy forehead gaze.

Clunk went her bracelets. Karen opened her eyes wide and gazed at Bella's forehead, and Bella dropped her head onto her desk, while her shoulders started heaving. Mrs. Hamilton had marched up to the back of the class as she was reading, and her long, full skirt swished around as she turned.

Two hundred to adore each breast

The words rang out richly, but at the word "breast" Bella cracked right out laughing. Mrs. Hamilton must have been expecting it, because she was right behind Bella's chair.

"Stand *up!*" she said, barking out *"up"* so loudly and suddenly that Bella was startled out of her giggles.

"Hold your head up, Bella," said Mrs. Hamilton. "I want everyone to see you. Now, then, how old are you?"

"Fifteen," said Bella, beginning to look sulky.

"Imagine that," said Mrs. Hamilton. "I thought perhaps you were thirteen and had gotten into this class by mistake."

She was terrific at sarcasm. I bet she'd wanted to go on the stage and her parents had said, "It's so uncertain, dear, better take a teaching diploma." Awful waste of talent, if you ask me. Bella was beginning to blush.

"And have you had the facts of life explained to you?" said Mrs. Hamilton. Her voice was all silky now. Sort of sweet and treacherous and sadistic, if you know what I mean.

"Yes, Mrs. Hamilton," said Bella.

"Oh?" said Mrs. Hamilton. "I thought perhaps you had culled all your information from the gutter press or the playground. I must have a word with whoever it is who does sex education with your class. Who is it, Bella?"

Bella mumbled.

"You've finished sex education? Perhaps I should arrange a refresher course in sex education for you." She was looking around the class as she spoke, obviously hoping we were admiring her performance and joining in with her against Bella. I thought that was going too far. It's one thing getting the better of someone who's being silly, but I don't see why she had to drag the rest of us into it. Everyone was feeling uneasy now and shuffling and looking down. Mrs. Hamilton sensed it. See what I mean about being the great actress who never was? She knew exactly how to play her audience. She knew how much we could take, and when she'd gone too far she back-pedaled. She stopped looking around, and her voice lost its heaviness and just became lightly ironic.

"I think perhaps, Bella," she said, "that in future we'll warn you if there's anything too mature in our poetry lessons, and you can go and join the eighth-graders for a while. Mm?"

Bella said nothing. Her face was dark red, and she was squirming inside.

"But on second thought, perhaps you'd like to have another chance at showing that you can cope with adult matters," said Mrs. Hamilton, and her voice had suddenly gone back to normal, nice and brisk and ordinary. It took the sting out of what she'd been saying.

"You can sit down now, you silly girl, and don't let it happen again."

And of course, it never did. After a week or two the effect wore off a bit, and Karen started nudging people when there was anything the slightest bit "rude," but Mrs. Hamilton only had to pause for a moment and put her head to one side in a questioning kind of way and give her one look, and Bella's knowing smile froze on her lips, and her giggle sort of died in her throat. By midterm, Mrs. Hamilton could declaim anything she liked and we were all carried away by it.

I would have thought that Miranda would have been one of the worst of the gigglers, but she wasn't. She'd changed since the summer vacation. She was much nicer. In fact, we'd become really good friends. Her parents had split up a few months earlier. Her mother had gone off to live with someone else, and she and her Dad had moved. They lived quite near us now. Miranda didn't talk about her parents much. She just said it had gotten easier, because, before, her parents had always had such awful fights, especially at night, and their apartment had been very small, and she'd heard every word, and her mother had never liked her much anyway. So now, at last, there was some peace and quiet.

I couldn't imagine what it would be like. I mean, I'd never imagined Mom and Dad splitting up or anything. They'd had fights, of course. In fact, they'd gotten worse recently. I could remember that a long time ago they'd seemed happier, before Mom became so tired with Ben and when Dad wasn't going away so much. But I'd never thought anything could go seriously wrong.

Miranda and I went home together most days now. There was often a wait for the bus, then quite a long walk at the end, so we had plenty of time to talk. I was horribly fascinated by her awful family. I could hardly believe some of the things she told me. But she seemed just as interested in mine.

"Hasn't your Mom ever tried to put Ben into a home?" she asked one day as we walked up the hill past the shops, lugging our great big bags full of the homework that Mrs. Hamilton had piled onto us.

"Of course not," I said scornfully. "She was upset when he was born, but she adores him now. Who wouldn't? I mean, you wouldn't put him in a home if he was yours, would you?"

Miranda had become one of Ben's biggest fans. She wasn't like Debbie, who took an intellectual interest in seeing how much he could learn. She just liked cuddling him and calling him silly names and talking baby talk. A normal two-year-old would have gotten bored and fed up probably, but Ben could go on being tickled and cuddled and cooed over forever.

"My Mom wouldn't even have brought him back from the hospital," said Miranda.

"Of course she would," I said, not really listening. I'd seen a boy in the distance, walking away from us, who looked a bit like Tony, and I watched hard till he turned down a side road. But then I saw his face and realized it was someone else. That happened about a hundred times a week, and I still hadn't gotten used to it.

"No, honestly," Miranda was saying. "She never wanted to have kids. Would you believe it, she even tried to have an abortion when she was expecting me? But it didn't work."

"What?" That stopped me dead in my tracks. I was listening hard enough now. "How do you know?"

"She told me one day when she was in an especially bad mood. She was sorry afterwards and said it wasn't true, but I know it was. I could *feel* it was."

Miranda shrugged as if she didn't care, but I could see the most awful pain in her face.

"My God," I said. I mean, what do you say when someone tells you a thing like that? That her own mother tried to get rid of her before she was born? "But she must have loved you and everything, once she actually saw you," I went on, feebly.

"Not really," said Miranda. "She did her duty by me, I suppose, but never anything extra. Not like your Mom. She really likes you. You can tell. Anyway"—she suddenly wanted to change the subject—"I don't care anymore. I'm grown up now. I don't need parents. I can look after myself. I'm going to be quite different from her. I'm going to have lots of babies, and I'm going to love them all."

"Yes," I said, "but mind you don't go and have one too soon by mistake." I didn't mean to sound nasty, but it came out all wrong. I was worried for a minute that I'd offended her, but that was one of the nicest things about Miranda. She didn't get upset easily. I suppose she'd had so many big things go wrong in her life that the little things didn't seem so bad. Anyway, she only laughed.

"I know what I'm doing," she said. "I take precautions."

I was dying of curiosity.

"D'you mean you're on the pill or something?" I said. "Have you really, I mean, done it, then?"

I wanted to ask her if she'd gone all the way, but I couldn't somehow bring it out. Miranda laughed and squeezed my arm.

"You've got a lot to learn, haven't you, Pee-wit?" she said, and I didn't notice till afterward that she hadn't answered my question.

"What's it like?" I said. I was desperate to know.

Miranda seemed to find it hard to put into words.

"It's just—it's cozy," she said. That wasn't at all what I was expecting. "When someone holds you, and you're close to them, snuggled right up, you feel all warm, and as if they loved you. Oh, I know they don't really. Boys are all the same. They just want to experiment and everything. But I don't mind if they do all that. Actually, I think it's rather boring. Overrated. I don't know what all the fuss is about. But it's so lovely having a boy have his arms around you and tell you how nice you are and sort of stroke you and everything. That's what I want. That's what I like."

Say what you like about Miranda, she's honest. I thought a lot about what she'd said when I got home. I felt I understood her now. I could see she'd been hungry for love all her life, and now she was being offered it, a kind of love anyway, so she was like a kid in a sweet shop, stuffing handfuls of goodies into her mouth. I'd always thought Miranda was so grown-up and sophisticated, but I suddenly saw that she was really a little girl wanting someone to cuddle her. I knew I didn't have to worry about her anymore, I mean, about myself not being as experienced as her and feeling silly and babyish and left behind. It would be different for me. Sort of holy and wild and all-consuming, like in *Wuthering Heights.* It wouldn't be boring for me. I felt quite sure of that.

I met Mom on the doorstep. She'd just gotten back from doing the shopping with Katy and Ben. I always like the days when she does a big grocery shopping at Safeway, because she can never resist the bakery counter and always brings back something sticky and sugary for tea. This time she had a bag of doughnuts.

"I must be crazy," she said, smiling fondly at Ben as he sat propped up on a cushion near the table smearing jam and sugar all over his face and mashing little bits of dough into the carpet.

"Who's the extra one for?" said Katy, looking at it greedily. It's so unfair the way that child stuffs herself and never seems to suffer for it. "She's a perfect little fairy," Dad says, in an unusual lapse from his normal perceptive self, and she's never had a pimple in her life. I should be so lucky.

"I thought Miranda might be here," said Mom. "She often drops in after school." I knew she was relieved to find me alone. Mom didn't like Miranda, any more than she'd liked Debbie. I know she thought she was a bad influence on me. It got me down. She ought to have known me better and trusted me a bit more. As if I'd start throwing myself at people, just through being friends with Miranda! I felt even more irritated now that I'd gotten to know her better. She needed someone like my mom to be nice to her, not to push her around.

"You're always on about Miranda," I blurted out,

knowing I was being unfair, because Mom hadn't actually said a word. "It's so mean. You don't know anything about her. She's got an awful home, and everyone's always criticizing her, and she needs all the friends she can get."

Mom seemed quite startled.

"You're a loyal little soul, aren't you, Annie?" she said. For a minute it sounded as if she was laughing at me. I knew she wasn't really, but I struck back before I could think.

"You're so intolerant!" I shouted. "You don't think anyone's worth anything unless they're ordinary and middle class and suburban like you!"

Katy went on unpacking the shopping bags with a revoltingly smug look on her face. Mom was quite mild, considering.

"Come off it, love," she said. "I just don't want you to pick up any of Miranda's bad habits, that's all."

I knew she was trying to be nice, but it's not easy to climb down off your high horse once you've climbed up onto it.

"How do you know," I said cuttingly, "that she isn't picking up any good habits from me, like loyalty, for example?" and I went out. I didn't slam the door, so Mom knew I wasn't really annoyed. Neither of us mentioned Miranda again during dinner, but I made a decision, a really definite decision, in the middle of the cauliflower gratin. If ever I fell in love and had a serious boyfriend, the last place I'd take him would be home. And that would serve my mother right for being so nasty about my friends.

Thinking about boyfriends set me off thinking about Tony, of course, and I couldn't concentrate on anything much for the rest of the evening. But later, after we'd watched a comedy show on TV and Katy had gone up to bed, Mom wanted to show me how tolerant she was, so she said why didn't I invite Miranda to help baby-sit Ben while she and Dad went to Auntie Janice's Saturday night. I bet she thought she was safe. She couldn't imagine Miranda not being booked up for a Saturday. But when I saw Miranda on the bus next morning, she said she'd love to come. She'd rather have a really chatty time with me and sit around cuddling Ben, she said. She was off boys for the time being anyway. So Mom got more than she bargained for. Miranda knew quite a lot about loyalty already.

I didn't let Mom know, but actually I was surprised that Miranda agreed to come on Saturday. It seemed so unlike her. She had never been known to spend Saturday night out of male company since that time when she was twelve and Kevin Gallagher took her to a party. She'd had too much to drink and done French kisses with Simon Petty, and on Monday morning at school, she'd described the whole thing, blow by blow, in the coatroom, while our eyes grew rounder and rounder. Since then, Miranda's Saturday nights had been a permanent source of entertainment on our Monday mornings.

When I opened the door to her, the children were already in bed, and Mom and Dad had gone out. She looked unlike herself. She hadn't done herself up, and she looked much younger and unglamorous and as if she could be easily hurt. I nearly said straight out, "You're not pregnant, are you?" but I managed not to.

She came in, took her shoes off straight away, and dropped down onto the sofa.

"Am I tired," she said. "I didn't get home till four this morning. Gary Fletcher's party."

"What did your dad say?" I said. "Mine goes up in smoke if I come home late."

"Dad!" she snorted. "He didn't come in himself till after six. He's in love. He's got a new girlfriend anyway."

I couldn't think of anything to say.

"Here, Anna," said Miranda, swiveling around on the sofa so that she could look at me properly. "Have you ever been in love?"

Luckily, I had turned at that very moment to put a cassette on, and I fiddled with the knobs on the loudspeaker to give myself time. I didn't want to talk about Tony. It was the deepest secret of my life. I felt that if I told anyone, it would escape from me and be tainted and sullied.

"What, me?" I said at last. "Don't be dumb."

It wasn't a lie exactly. I've had to give up telling lies, because I can't carry it off. I look self-conscious and give the game away. Miranda didn't notice anything. She was used to me running myself down. She had only asked the question to give herself the chance to talk anyway.

"Because I'm in love," she said, and she threw her arms above her head and wiggled her toes down the sofa under one of the cushions and gave a huge sigh. It's a funny thing, but during all those years that Miranda had been messing around with boys and saying how crazy she was about Ted or Tom or Matthew, and swooning over their eyes or their cool jackets or their glitzy motorbikes or something, I'd never once heard her actually say she was in love.

"Who with?" I said. And then all of a sudden I was wary. I knew what she was going to say before she said it.

"Can't you guess?" She smiled up at me. Her eyes were wide open. They looked neater without the crust of makeup that was usually caked all around them.

"You met him," she went on. "You know. Down at Ted's when we were all playing tennis. That wonderful tall boy with the dark hair. Tony. Come on, Anna. You remember!"

"Oh, him!" I said, and even though my throat had gone tight, I managed to sound halfway normal. I couldn't look down into her face any longer without feeling like a traitor. I don't know why I felt guilty, because I hadn't done anything at all, but you can't help your feelings. I went into the kitchen, wanting to hide my face, which I knew was turning red.

"I'll get us a Coke," I said, and clattered around pretending to look in all the cupboards to give my face time to fade.

"Did you see him again?" I called out. It was easier to talk at a distance. "Where did you meet him in the first place, anyway?" I waited, breathless with anxiety.

"That's the funny thing," Miranda said. "I'd only met him that morning. He knows Joe a bit. And I never even saw him again after that day. He went off, do you remember, when your Mom arrived, and I was too thick

to run after him and get his telephone number. I asked
Joe about him, but he says he hasn't been around for a
while and he doesn't even know his surname, let alone
where he's gone, and oh, Anna, I've never felt like this
before! I'd do anything to get him. I can't be bothered to
go out with all those silly little boys anymore. What's
the point? I keep after Joe for his address, but he says he
doesn't know anything else about him. I think he's bluff-
ing. He's jealous, because he wants me himself. But I'll
get hold of Tony if it's the last thing I do," and she
gripped a cushion between two clenched fists and let out
a sort of animal cry, then punched it furiously away
from her.

My heart sank into my boots. Once Miranda had
her hooks into Tony, there was no more to be said. She
had a way of going after a boy that no one had ever been
known to resist. She was fearless, shameless, ruthless,
single-minded, and ready to do anything anyone
wanted. I hadn't got a chance.

At that moment there was a sudden wail upstairs.

"I'll go," said Miranda, jumping up, instantly forget-
ting the pangs of unrequited love. "I'll bring him down,
shall I?"

"Okay, if you like," I said. Mom didn't like Ben
coming down in the evening. She said it spoiled him and
he'd get into the habit, and then we'd never get him to
go to sleep, but I knew Miranda was dying to cuddle him
and I didn't have the will to resist her. I was too preoccu-
pied. My mind was spinning around, out of control, trying to grab hold of what she'd told me.

A minute later she was downstairs again with Ben in

her arms. She put him down on the sofa and let her hair flop onto his face.

"Agoo," she said.

Ben screamed with laughter and tried to catch hold of her hair with his little hands, but he was always just too slow as Miranda flicked it out of reach.

"Who cares about silly old boys?" she said in the special, soppy voice she always used with Ben. "Miranda loves babies, yes she does. Miranda's going to have lots of ickle pickle babies and she's going to cuddle them all day long."

"When you've quite finished," I said, knowing I sounded a bit ratty, but not bothering to hide it, "I'll give him his drink." And I pushed her out of the way, picked Ben up off the sofa, and settled him on my knee, where he drank noisily out of his cup.

Miranda might stand the best chance with Tony, but nobody would ever take Ben away from me, I thought.

Seven

Not long after the beginning of the term, ben went into the hospital. He'd been in before, several times, like when they'd put a little drain thing in to take some of the fluid off his head and when he'd had other things wrong, like bronchitis, that normal babies would have shaken off quite easily.

"Just routine," Dr. Randall said, but I didn't believe him. For one thing, Mom seemed so down about it. I caught the end of what she was saying on the phone when I got in from school.

". . . don't think they'll operate again. It's too risky. It's the heart problem, too, I think."

She sighed, and paused, and I could hear a sort of quacking, crackling sound, which was Aunty Janice answering. Aunty Janice talks so loudly over the phone you have to hold the receiver about half a mile away from your ear if you don't want to get your eardrums blasted.

"Oh no," Mom went on. "*He's* not here. You might have guessed that. I sometimes think . . ." and then I

7 8

saw her looking at me, and I knew she wanted to talk about Dad but wasn't going to till I was out of the way.

It was true. Dad wasn't at home much now. And it wasn't just that he went away so much, he'd sort of changed when he was home too. When he'd first got his traveling job, it had been wonderful every time he came back. Funny, and special. Like Christmas. But that was all over now. He didn't kind of clown around anymore and make a fuss of us like he used to.

I blamed Mom. She was so tight and sort of prickly and miserable. She'd wither him up with a look if he started being playful, and then she'd sigh and say something like, "It's all very well you being so cheerful. You're not stuck here all the time with a sick kid and no one to talk to," and I'd feel insulted, because she'd called me "no one," and Dad would look guilty and irritated at the same time.

I hated hearing Mom going on and on about Dad to Aunty Janice. I'm never going to do that if I get married, talk about my husband to other people, I mean. It's sneaky. So I went into the kitchen and made a bit of noise getting myself a cup of tea, so that she'd be sort of reminded that I was there and perhaps that might stop her from being disloyal. And I was just wondering what I could do next to get her off the phone, when the doorbell rang.

The phone in our house is in the hall, right by the front door, and I heard Mom say quickly, "Sorry, Jan, got to go," and click the receiver down. Then I heard the door open and Mom's voice go really polite and a bit smarmy.

"Oh hello, Mr. Henderson, do come in. How nice of you to call."

It was the minister.

We're not exactly what you'd call a churchy family. We only used to go at Christmas and Easter and christenings and things. But Mom had taken to going more often, and sometimes I went with her. I couldn't decide whether I liked it or not. Church made me swing violently from one mood to another. I either felt exalted and holy and full of goodwill toward men, or I was bored and grumpy and supercritical.

I didn't mind Mr. Henderson usually. He was just middle-aged and ordinary. But I didn't want to see him that day, because Mom had dragged Katy and me off to the harvest festival a couple of weeks earlier, and Mr. Henderson had stopped me at the church door.

"Well, well," he'd said. "It's Anna, isn't it?" and he'd taken my hand to shake it and didn't seem about to let it go again. "And how are you, young lady?"

I muttered something. I wanted to say, "Fine thanks, old gentleman," but of course I didn't. My life is littered with wasted opportunities. And anyway, I liked Mr. Henderson.

"Have we seen you at our youth club yet?" he went on.

"No," I said uncomfortably. I was beginning to feel trapped.

"Come next week, then," he said. I'll say one thing for him. He had the trick of speaking intensely to you, as if you were all alone, even though half a million people were milling around, trampling on his surplice, trying to

barge in and ask him idiotic questions about choir practice or make personal criticisms of his sermon or moan on about what agony their piles were or something.
"What do you say, then?" he asked, still gazing at me intently. "Friday at seven-thirty at the rectory. Will you come?"

"All right," I'd said weakly, and he'd let go of my hand and turned to the next person and was quickly engulfed in a sea of blue rinses.

I hoped the whole thing would be quietly forgotten. The last thing I wanted to do was go to some sweaty youth club with a lot of horrible pimply kids years younger than me. So I stood in the kitchen, being quiet and hoping they wouldn't come in. But of course Mom had to go and offer Mr. Henderson a cup of tea, and he had to go and accept, so they both came in and caught me.

"Sorry we didn't see you on Friday," said Mr. Henderson, all bright and breezy. "How about this week?"

"Well, I don't . . ." I mumbled, trying to edge toward the door.

"It's very kind of you to think of Anna," said Mom with that little shrill laugh she gives when she's embarrassed. "Of course you'll be there on Friday, won't you, Anna?"

I gave her the dirtiest look I dared in front of the minister.

"You might meet some really nice young people for a change," said Mom, rather meaningfully.

I knew she meant "boys" but didn't dare say so. I could read her mind like a book. Boys at church would be safe and well-behaved and respectable, not a rough, tough lot like Miranda's.

In the end, I went. There was no way out. I might have gotten away with it if Mr. Henderson hadn't had a surprising burst of memory for such a white-haired old gent, but he phoned Mom the next day and said how much he was looking forward to seeing me on Friday, so that put the lid on it.

Actually, I was pleasantly surprised. I grumbled like mad about going, of course, but it wasn't at all bad. The rectory was a funny old house with a vast basement that Mr. Henderson had turned into a game room. It was really good. I'd thought it would be all holy and embarrassing, but the only holy bit was a prayer at the end, and I didn't mind that too much. Apart from that, all we did was play table tennis (and I'm brilliant at that), and Mr. Henderson showed us how to score properly at darts. Most of the kids there didn't even go to church, or not much anyway. They just liked the group and Mr. Henderson. There were quite a few younger ones, but they mostly watched cartoons on the television. There were several others of my age, including a girl named Diana, that I quite liked, and a boy named Jeff, who was a real comedian. He had bubbly blond hair and a cheeky grin and a sort of bouncy, nice, funny way of walking. When he got going doing his imitation of TV personalities and making us guess who was who, we rolled around the floor laughing. He was brilliant as Mr. Henderson. Jeff wasn't the romantic-hero type, like Tony, but I could imagine myself being good friends with him. He didn't scare me. He had this fantastic knack of making really

witty remarks all the time, like when Mr. Henderson
said, "I don't know how you do it, Jeff, getting your Dad
to lend you his car all the time. It's all right for some,"
and Jeff answered, quick as a flash, "Where there's a will,
there's relations."

I could tell Jeff liked me a bit. He kept fixing it so
that we'd be paired off at table tennis. It was probably
only because I was good at it, and it gave him a better
chance of winning, but I sort of knew it was because of
me too. I was looking my best that evening, giving off
the odd electric flash, I was sure. I hadn't felt that way
for ages.

I had to eat humble pie at home and say I rather
liked youth club and that I'd go again next week. In fact,
it wasn't bad to have somewhere to go on a Friday night,
because for years I'd been the only girl in class, I was
sure, who had nothing to do but sit at home and do even
more homework or watch boring sitcoms on TV. I'd felt
like a real freak, left out.

Jeff wasn't there the third time I went. Nor was Diana. I was disappointed. The sparkle had gone out of the
evening. I played a bit of table tennis and talked to a boy
named Sam, but he was really boring. He had those red
clammy hands that he kept twisting around, as if he was
washing them. I was trying to shake him off when the
phone rang. Mr. Henderson answered it. He wrote something down on a scrap of paper.

"It's for you, Anna," he said, handing it to me. That
was just like Mr. Henderson. He could have shouted out
my personal business in front of everyone and made me

look an idiot, but instead he was wonderfully matter-of-fact and mature about it all.

The note just said, "Anna—please meet Jeff at the station 9:30 after club."

I couldn't believe it. A date! I felt myself going red, then shivery. Thank God I'd washed my hair before I'd gone out, and had put on my best sweatshirt. Trust Jeff to do things differently, I thought. It was such a funny way to ask me out, through Mr. Henderson and everything. I hadn't realized he'd liked me that much. I hadn't realized things had gone that far. I phoned Mom, said I'd be home late, and left club early. It was a good fifteen-minute walk to the station, but I wanted to have plenty of time. I had to sort things out in my mind.

It was funny, but having a real date with a real person made Tony seem farther away and less interesting. I knew it would be good fun going out with Jeff. There'd be lots of laughs, and I was pretty sure we'd like doing the same kinds of things, but I could have serious conversations with him, too, if we both felt in the mood. I would feel a bit strange at first because I wasn't used to going out with boys, but I wouldn't be paralyzed with nerves like I would have been if Tony had asked me out. Actually, the more I thought about it, the more I liked Jeff's face better than Tony's, or what I could remember of Tony's. He was more my kind of person, somehow.

It was a funny way, though, to ask a girl out with you. I couldn't really see why he hadn't asked Mr. Henderson if he could speak to me. But then I felt glad that he'd done it like this, without giving me time to think about it or the chance to say no. I'd have gotten all stewed up if I'd had more warning.

I hadn't been to the station in the evening very often before. It was surprisingly busy. There were a lot of people waiting, meeting friends, I suppose, or just hanging around. I was early. I couldn't see Jeff anywhere, so I stood near the do-it-yourself photo machine and waited.

I saw him at last, after what seemed a lifetime but was really only ten minutes. He was wearing a shabby old bomber jacket and didn't look like his usual spruce, sparky self. He was grubby, as if he'd been doing a dirty job, and looked tired. I was just about to go up to him, when I went hot and cold all over. Diana had appeared from the other end of the entrance hall.

"Jeff!" I heard her call. He turned and started toward her.

"Hi!" he called back. Light dawned. With a sickening thud I realized the truth. They had obviously come to meet each other. The message must have been for "Diana," not for "Anna." Mr. Henderson had made a ridiculous, stupid blunder. As luck would have it, I was standing right between them. They were both coming toward me. Any minute now they'd be bound to see me. I turned in panic and bolted into the photograph booth. Thank goodness, it was empty.

I heard them stop right outside and actually saw their feet from behind the skimpy green curtain. I was nearly dying of shame. Supposing Diana recognized my shoes? She'd admired them only last week. She'd never have the chance again. I'd never have the nerve to go

back to the youth club after this. I curled my feet away
from the opening as far out of sight as possible.

"Glad you got my message," Jeff was saying. He
sounded rushed and not particularly welcoming.

"Dad gave it to me," said Diana. "I got home late
from swimming."

"He thought you were at the youth club," said Jeff.
"I phoned there, too, and left a message for you. Funny.
Mr. Henderson said you were there."

"Oh well," said Diana. "You know what he's like.
He can be a bit vague sometimes. Let's get going. I don't
want to be too late tonight. Where's the stuff?"

"It's out the back, in Dad's car," said Jeff. "We'll
have to make a couple of trips. I'm beginning to regret
volunteering for this. I've been at it all evening. I've just
about had rummage sales."

Their voices moved away and merged with the
thundering of a train pounding through the station.

I sat there, quite motionless, for a good five minutes.
I had never felt like such a fool in all my life.

"Serves you right," I kept saying to myself. "Serves
you bloody well right." I don't know why I was so angry
with myself. I suppose I should have blamed Mr. Henderson. But it isn't easy being furious with him. Anger
doesn't sort of stick to him, if you know what I mean.

It was quite a long walk home, and as I went, I began to feel better. At least they hadn't seen me. And I
hadn't let on to Mom. I just said I'd be late. The chances
were that Mr. Henderson wouldn't remember a thing
about it. His memory, though very good in some ways,
was selective. The only person who knew what a fool I

was, was me. And I knew that anyway. Perhaps I would go back to the club next week, after all.

I'd learned something about myself as well. Thinking about Jeff had put Tony out of my mind, and if I could forget him so easily, perhaps I wasn't in love with him at all.

Eight

THE WORST THING ABOUT STARTING A NEW YEAR AT SCHOOL IS that you always have to work a bit harder. You finish up at the end of the summer term sure that you'll die if you ever have to go through exams again, but lo and behold, come the start of autumn, there you are again. Once school had gotten going, I found myself doing so much homework I'd have to stagger back every day, weighted down with half the school library in my bag. I never used most of the books, but I was so neurotic in case I needed to look something up and didn't have it with me that I used to overdo it and take far too many home just to be on the safe side. It's a wonder that I didn't end up with a permanent curvature of the spine.

Miranda didn't bother about work much, and the sickening thing was that she did nearly as well as me. She had a natural thing for languages. She could prattle away in French and German with an amazingly convincing accent, while I was still stuck, plowing through lists of irregular verbs and getting dreadfully muddled up with them all. Anyway, you can't really make yourself better at languages. You can either do them or you can't. But with history and English literature and all the stuff I cared most about, you have to wade through tons of books if you want to write a decent essay.

I'd had enough of Miranda, actually. It was mainly because she bored on and on about Tony all the time. I thought about him a lot still, in spite of the jolt I'd received when I thought Jeff was asking me out, but I knew it was unreal. I never expected to see him again. He was just the person I daydreamed about, like I used to about Miss Winter. But Miranda kept on about strategy, about how she'd hang about near the tennis courts when the good weather started again, in case he came back there, and how she'd invite him to such and such a party, or make sure her dad was out and get him to come around to her flat. She'd have done it, too, I know she would, if Tony had shown up again. I didn't like the thought of it. If Miranda was really in love, the real thing, I mean, I didn't think she ought to stoop to sordid schemes. Her craze for Tony hadn't even stopped her carrying on with other boys. She was just the same as ever, always slipping out of school at lunchtime to meet someone down at the station snackbar. She even boasted about having an affair with a ticket collector. And she was forever mooning around with Joe in the new McDonald's that had opened up on Main Street.

I didn't invite her home very often now. It wasn't only because I'd gone off her a bit. It was also because of Mom. Once Ben was back home from the hospital, she'd become more difficult than ever. Dad and I had had a very mature discussion about it on one of the weekends when he was at home. He said she was depressed, and we had to be very understanding, and she'd get better in time, and he was trying to get her to go to the doctor's, but I noticed he didn't stick around to make sure she went.

To be fair, Mom had an awful lot to do with Ben. The older he got, the more he needed looking after. He seemed to sleep even less at night, and he was a weight to carry around. Even ordinary things like changing his diaper and getting him up into his chair to feed him were an effort. You had to really heave to lift him off the ground. Then, I suppose, Mom had to keep up with the house and everything. She didn't have to do much for me, of course. Being fifteen, I was practically grown up, and less dependent on home. I could look after myself, thank you very much. But Katy still needed a lot of maternal love. I'd gotten quite fond of Katy, actually. She was turning out to be a rather nice person. She'd dropped a lot of her babyish ways and was quite good company sometimes. We still had fights, of course, like when she borrowed my parrot pin without asking me, for her school Christmas party, and it got broken when she fell off her chair in musical chairs, but on the whole, we didn't get on too badly.

Katy's birthday is in October. On October 21st, in fact, the same day as Queen Victoria's, as she never fails to tell anybody who will listen. You'd have thought no one else in the world knew what birthdays are, the way Katy goes on about hers. She starts in about June every year, saying things to her friends like, "If you don't lend me your new ballet shoes, you won't be invited to my party." It never fails.

It was that, though, that led to all the trouble. Mom came upon Katy writing out for the tenth time the list of kids she wanted to invite, crossing out Tracey because they'd had an argument and putting back Stewart because he'd given her a fruit gum during lunch break, and Mom said, "You're not expecting a party this year, are you? I couldn't possibly manage it, what with Ben being in and out of the hospital and everything. Anyway, I thought you'd grown out of that kind of thing."

Katy couldn't believe her ears. She'd been thinking about nothing else for weeks. The fact that Mom hadn't noticed shows just how remote she had become. Everyone else was sick to death of the subject. Katy went white, then red, and shouted at Mom that she was an old cow and ran out of the kitchen, stamping up the stairs so hard that the whole house shook. I expected Mom to fly after her and give her a scolding. She doesn't allow such language. But she just sat down at the kitchen table and put her head in her hands. I was about to stick my oar in and say something really cutting, because I'd had a great party when I was ten and I thought she was being too hard on Katy, when I suddenly took pity on her. Her shoulders were drooping, and her hair looked straggly, and I could see that she was tired, all the way through, right down to her bones. So I said, and I think I was very dignified and adult about it, "She's got her heart set on it, Mom. I think, in all fairness, we'll have to do it."

Mom didn't move. I had that awful feeling I get when the class is dead quiet and Mrs. Gordon asks for volunteers to do some poisonous job, like setting out the chairs in the hall for a parents' evening or selling tickets for the school concert. I'm always the dope who volunteers. I don't know why, I just seem to be propelled forward by an alien force, and before I know where I am, I'm landed with it. So I heard myself saying, without quite knowing how or why, "You can leave the whole thing to me, Mom. I'll organize a disco for Katy and buy some Coke and hamburgers, and you needn't lift a finger. We'll do it next weekend, when Dad's at home. He can be the disc jockey."

She looked at me then.

"I can't stand the noise," she said, and there was a kind of desperation in her voice, "and kids traipsing in and out, and Ben getting out of his routine, and the mess . . ."

I started feeling annoyed then.

"Look," I said, and I know I sounded exasperated. "It's the kid's birthday. She's ten years old. She's told her friends. You can't let her down."

She went on staring at me, helplessly.

"Ben can go to Aunty Janice," I said. "She's always offering to have him. And you can go out for the afternoon. We can manage quite well without you," and I didn't realize until later that it must have sounded cruel.

I rather enjoyed setting up Katy's disco. For one thing, she was desperately grateful. She hung on my arm when we went down to the toy store to choose some party favors. I told her she could spend a dollar on each kid, and she chose the weirdest things, like rainbow notepads and revolting pencils with pink and yellow teddies on them. Still, I suppose a child's taste is bound to be rather naive. I seem to remember liking the most grotesque pictures of long-eared dogs with enormous teardrops in their eyes when I was her age. She'll grow out of it one day.

I knew exactly how to organize the food. I'd had to do the hamburger and hot-dog stand at the school Christmas fair. It had been a worry beforehand, but it had gone beautifully, and Miss Winter had said I had a natural talent for administration. A disco for ten little kids was nothing in comparison with that. The hardest part, strangely enough, was persuading Dad to be a disc jockey. I never thought he'd be difficult about giving Katy a birthday party, but he seemed to think that Mom was really unwell, and that it would be too much for her, and that she needed as much peace and quiet as she could get.

"Well, why don't you stay home a bit more," I burst out, "and take the strain off her?"

Dad wasn't angry. His face just closed up, and he said he didn't think he'd be of any use. He didn't seem to be able to say the right thing, ever, these days. In the end, though, he decided it might be a good idea, and he agreed to help, so we wrote "six to eight" on the invitations to keep it down to only two hours, and Mom said okay, but would we please make sure that the music wasn't turned up so loud that the pictures would be shaken off the walls.

I sometimes have an uncanny feeling that Katy's really the older one of us two. She's certainly got an ad-

vanced sense of fashion and style, much better than
mine. I look quite good these days, even if I do say so
myself, now that the braces are off my teeth and I keep
my lenses in all the time and the pimples are clearing up
(except for the odd one on my chin). But Katy's a natural. She spends hours in front of her mirror in her room
twisting an old scarf around her head and looking at it
from all angles, or trying on different things with each
other to see how they look. I must admit, she gets results.
She's a ten-year-old knockout. I bet she'll be a model or
a dress designer or something when she grows up.

She saved up several weeks' worth of pocket money
before the disco and spent most of it on makeup. I wasn't
sure if she should be allowed to. I mean, a ten-year-old
dolled up to the eyebrows seems a bit obscene to me. I
never even thought of it at her age. I was much too sensible.

When the day finally came, she didn't let me see her
getting ready for the party. I suppose she thought I'd
object. When I did see her at last, I nearly burst out
laughing, which, I have learned from long experience,
would have been fatal.

She was wearing a sugar-pink jumpsuit, and orange
Robin Hood boots, and she'd rolled a crimson scarf with
sparkly fringes into a rope and tied it around her forehead. So far so good. A bit on the bright side, perhaps,
but within limits. But it was her makeup that knocked
me out. I mean, pink and orange hairspray in stripes (a
bit wobbly down the back) and gelled so that it stuck out
all over, and red eyeshadow, and black lipstick . . .

I opened my mouth, then saw the expression on her face. It was sort of hopeful, and pleading.

"You look great," I said. "Fantastic. Super cool."

She did a pirouette and danced off to show Mom. And Mom actually laughed, a nice laugh, not a sarcastic one. It was such a surprise to hear it that I knew Katy wouldn't take offense. Then I heard Mom say, "You look wonderful, darling. However do you do it? Whatever will you think up next?" And I felt that perhaps there was hope, that we might one day turn back into a proper, nice family again, with an ordinary mom who did things with us.

Once Katy's friends arrived, I didn't have time to turn around, let alone notice what any of them was wearing. I began to see why Mom had made such a fuss about having the disco in the first place. The noise was horrific. Those ten kids sounded like fifty. They got so excited, they shrieked for the full two hours, at the tops of their voices, almost drowning out the music, which Katy had turned up as high as she dared.

I don't know, quite honestly, how much Katy enjoyed it. She seemed tense most of the time. She kept trying to organize the others into partners and wandering into the kitchen to ask when tea would be ready and making Dad stop the record in the middle to announce a competition for the best makeup. I think she found the whole thing a bit of a strain.

Tracey didn't help. She'd been invited after all, since she and Katy had officially been best friends for years and years, but she was mean all the time, ostentatiously ignoring Katy and going around with Stewart, who had a slick hairstyle and a sensational wiggle in his hips when he danced. It was Debbie and me and Emma all over again, and my heart bled for Katy. It needn't have. I've got to hand it to her, that kid's brilliant at getting what she wants. She wangled it very neatly so that Stewart sat next to her at tea, and she managed to palm Tracey off onto Conrad, a funny kid with a brush of stiff, carroty hair. Then all through tea she whispered funny, catty things to Stewart about Tracey, and Stewart laughed so much he choked on a potato chip. I could see Tracey going wild with jealousy. In the end she couldn't stand it any longer and came to try to get Stewart to dance with her again in the other room, but she timed it all wrong, because he was after a second bit of birthday cake, and Katy had promised him the slice with the most M & M's on it. So Tracey wandered off, rejected, and Katy won hands down. Good for her. I wish I'd been so clever over that sneaky Emma.

Mom stayed in bed most of the afternoon. She said she had a headache. But she popped down once or twice and smiled at the milling mob of children. And when they'd all gone, and I'd flopped down, exhausted, onto the sofa, with empty potato chip bags and birthday wrapping paper crunching under me every time I moved, I could hear her in the kitchen with Dad.

They were in there for a long time. I thought I heard her cry and then Dad talking softly and then, ages later, I heard them moving around and water running and everything, and Mom's voice was louder and natural, even happy. And I heard her laugh out loud, in a way that I hadn't heard for ages.

"Well done, Annie," she said to me later that evening. "You did manage without me very well. But I don't think you'll have to next time. I don't think I'm quite ready for you to take this family over yet. Especially not now that Dad's going to change his job. He's putting in for a transfer so that he won't have to travel so much. Think of all the shirts I'll have to iron again!" and she smiled as if she didn't know perfectly well that I knew perfectly well that she hated ironing more than anything else in the world.

Mom didn't get better overnight, but she did start being a bit more normal after that. I don't know what she and Dad had said in the kitchen, but the stupid walls they'd built up between themselves had come down again. Dad was still going to go away a lot for a couple of months, but there was light at the end of the tunnel. He'd soon be back home, and then he'd be here for good.

I don't want to boast, but I think I was the one who got it sorted out. I don't mean Dad changing his job. I think he must have decided that by himself. I mean, me doing the disco for Katy made Mom wake up to the fact that she had got other kids besides Ben. I didn't mind her spending most of her time with him, except when she sort of squeezed me out of the way, like when he was ill and she wouldn't let anyone else cuddle him, even though I was sure he'd have preferred me sometimes. But what I did mind was that she seemed to give Katy a whole lot more time than she was prepared to give me. I know I'm too old, really, to need a mother much, but I did feel pardonably annoyed when Mom found time to take Katy ice-skating but couldn't be bothered to go shopping with me. It started nagging at me after a bit, and I got to the point where I noticed every tiny thing she said to Katy, and I brooded about it afterward.

I suppose it had to boil up eventually. In the end it was something really silly that set it off.

I was in the school play. It wasn't a speaking part or anything. I was just a guest at a party in *Lady Windermere's Fan.* I love Oscar Wilde. It makes me feel languorous, and sophisticated, and unspeakably elegant. Mrs. Hamilton was directing the play, of course, and she and Miss Macfarlane, the home economics teacher, provided the basic costume, but I had to dress it up with extras, like a collar and costume jewelry and long gloves and things. When Mrs. Hamilton mentioned collars, I remembered that Mom had a wonderful lace one tucked away in her underwear drawer. It was real, good old lace. Her grandmother had given it to her years ago. She'd never once used it. In fact, I only knew it was there because I'd helped her tidy her drawers one day when I was home from school with a cold, and I'd found it. But would she lend it me for the school play? Would she ever! It was too precious, she said. I might lose it, or cut it by mistake, or get it covered with makeup.

"Or it might get eaten by the school cat," I said angrily. "I do know how to take care of things, you know. Why won't you let me? It's not doing any good moldering away in your drawer."

But Mom was adamant. There was nothing I could do but buy a cheap piece of white eyelet embroidery in

Woolworth's and tack that on instead. It didn't look half as good.

And then—and *then*—the Saturday before the play, I met Katy flouncing downstairs with Mom's best hat that she wore to Cousin Julia's wedding stuck on her head. I couldn't believe my eyes. I was cut to the heart. I pushed past Katy and tore up to Mom's bedroom. She was tidying out her wardrobe.

"It's not fair," I yelled at her. "Katy gets whatever she wants. She only has to lift a finger. But I want something for serious educational purposes and you couldn't care less. I've had enough. I'm taking it, whatever you say," and I darted over to Mom's chest of drawers and wrenched open the drawer and dragged out the collar and stood there, glaring at her, my chest heaving with emotion and, I felt quite sure, my eyes flashing magnificently.

"Put it down at once," my mother said sharply, and I could see that she was really annoyed.

"Why should I?" I said. "You've given Katy your best hat just to play with."

I saw light dawn in Mom's face and the anger melted out of it.

"Annie," she said, in her irritatingly understanding voice. "Do you know how much that collar is worth?"

"No," I said, feeling suddenly unsure of myself. I had never thought of it as having a value, in money I mean.

"At least a hundred dollars," she said, "unless you've just torn it."

"What?" I gasped. I suddenly felt as if the thing in

my hands was red hot. I put it gently down on her dressing table.

"Why didn't you tell me before?" I said. "I'm quite capable of understanding things, you know, if they're properly explained to me."

"I know, darling," she said, and I heard a hint of laughter in her voice. I suppose I did sound rather funny. Wounded dignity sort of thing.

"Well anyway," I said, feeling on safer ground, "I still don't see why Katy should have your best hat." She laughed out loud at that.

"Best?" she said. "Have you looked at it lately? It's got a hole the size of a quarter in the brim. It's not exactly new, you know. Julia's been married for five years. They've got two children already. Anyway, I won't need a hat for years. The next wedding I go to will probably be yours."

"Don't be silly, Mom," I said. "No one will ever want to marry me."

"Oh yes they will," she said. "I've noticed lately that you're looking very pretty these days. I've been sorting through some fabric this afternoon. I thought you might like me to make you a dress."

It was a nice thought of Mom's, and I appreciated the offer, but I was slightly taken aback at the same time. Mom can get very enthusiastic about sewing when she gets going, which isn't very often, but the results are patchy, to say the least. Occasionally she produces a real knockout, but more often than not, it doesn't fit and the seams are a bit puckered, and the hem wobbles up and down. I looked at the fabric she'd dug out. It was all several years old, and in colors that no one would be seen dead in now. But I was so happy I didn't care. Mom wanted to make me something. Mom thought I was pretty. Ben and Katy weren't the only ones Mom loved.

"And anyway," I said to myself afterward, when I had time to think, "I don't have to wear it very often."

I made a sudden decision. It was time I got a Saturday job. Emma and Vicky were both working at Tesco's on the weekend. I could do the same. I could start making some real money myself, and then I'd be able to buy my own clothes for a change.

Nine

In the end I didn't get a job at tesco's. they told me they didn't need anyone. I think Emma sabotaged my chances, actually. She shrieked when she saw me coming for an interview and said, right in front of the supervisor, "Oh, look! It's Pea-brain! Don't worry, Pea-brain, we won't let on. We won't tell them the truth about you. Ha ha!" and then she dug Vicky in the ribs. The supervisor turned around and gave me a dirty look and was very stiff and starchy in the interview. I knew I wasn't going to get in before she even told me. Vicky didn't help. She just smirked. I didn't blame her, though. She's so used to being on the receiving end of Emma's nastiness, I suppose it made a change to be ganging up with her on someone else. But I could have strangled Emma. There are no limits to that girl's malice.

I went off home and stopped at Mrs. Chapman's to get a package of envelopes. I felt sure I was going to have to write a lot of applications. But there was a lovely surprise waiting for me.

"Writing love letters, I suppose?" said Mrs. Chapman, nodding and winking at me so that her double chins bounced up and down as she took my money. You mind when some people tease you, but you'd never mind with Mrs. Chapman. She's got such a nice nature herself that she only laughs if anyone makes fun of her, and her attitude sort of rubs off onto other people.

"Funny kind of love letters," I said. "I'm looking for a Saturday job. I'm going to write to a few places."

"You want to work Saturdays?" said Mrs. Chapman. She looked thoughtful.

"Yes," I said. "Half the girls at school do, and I'd like to have some money of my own for a change. I'd like to get myself a few things to wear and save up for when I go skiing with the school next year."

"Where are they working, then, your friends?" said Mrs. Chapman.

"Oh, just Tesco's and McDonald's, and the garden center down Stack's Lane," I said.

"How much do you get in Tesco's?" she asked.

I told her.

"That's fair," she said. "Look, Anna, why don't you work for me? I'll give you the same. I could use some help Saturdays. It's always busy in here. My poor old legs kill me, what with jumping up and down every five minutes to get something off the high shelves. I can't get around like I used to."

I couldn't believe it.

"You don't mean it, do you, Mrs. Chapman?" I said. "You can't be serious?"

"Course I'm serious," she said. "I wouldn't joke

about something like that. When do you want to start? Now?"

"I'd better just pop home and tell Mom," I said. "She's expecting me back at lunchtime."

"Give her a ring," said Mrs. Chapman. "There's a phone through the back there," and she lifted up the flap in the counter and stood back to let me through.

I've been going into that shop ever since I can remember, but never, not in my wildest dreams, did I imagine that I'd be allowed past the counter, under the magic flap, to see the mysteries behind. It's funny, when you think about it, how many things in this life you never notice. I mean, I've been walking down our Main Street for years, but I never looked up above the shop fronts till the other day. I was quite surprised. The buildings were interesting, all in different styles, and some had windows with proper curtains and window boxes full of flowers on the sills. I suppose they must be apartments. I'd always thought Main Street was just shops. After that I noticed front doors squeezed in between the shop fronts. I must have been blind as a bat not to notice them before.

It was nice in behind Mrs. Chapman's. She had a sort of living room cum storeroom, with a few comfy chairs, a gas fire, a place to make tea, and a lot of boxes full of Mars bars and things. I'd never thought of her as living anywhere, really. She just seemed to belong behind her counter, but she told me later that she had a nice bungalow on the main road, handy for the buses. I felt nervous, that first Saturday morning, standing behind the counter. Fortunately I'd been in the shop so often I knew where most things were. Mrs. Chapman gave me a blue-checked nylon smock to wear, and it's funny, but once I had it on, I felt official and in charge. The customers treated me differently too. Most people didn't look at me properly, I mean as myself, Anna Peacock. They saw my smock, realized I was an assistant, and stared through me or past me. It was, "Couple of packages of potato chips and a *TV Times* please," or "Is this week's *Woman* in yet?"

You had to have a lot of patience. I remember thinking years ago that you had to have a butterfly mind to work in a shop. I don't think that anymore. You just need to be able to keep your temper, have a good pair of legs, and eyes in the back of your head.

I got annoyed with the children sometimes. They were so noisy and pushy, never letting anyone else get near the counter. And they'd stand there, with a quarter in their hands, taking half an hour to choose one chocolate bar, making you tell them the prices over and over again. Mrs. Chapman was ever so good with them. I tried to be. She told me I'd been just the same when I was a kid. She could see me now, trying to decide whether to spend my pocket money on a bouncy rubber ball or a stick of licorice as if my life depended on it. I don't believe I was as bad as those kids, though. For one thing, I was never that cheeky.

Some of the old people were nice. They tended to notice me more and be polite. They liked to stop for a chat. But there were a few that needed careful handling. One old lady came in to buy a birthday card for her brother. Mrs. Chapman gave me a little shove toward the card rack when she saw her coming.

"You'd better go and give her a hand," she whispered. "Poor old girl's often in here. She doesn't know the time of day no more."

She was right.

"I'm looking for a birthday card," the old lady said brightly, "for my brother." She'd pulled a card out of the rack already. It said, "For a boy who's seven" on it.

"How old is your brother?" I said.

"That's none of your business," she snapped. I looked around at Mrs. Chapman. I was beginning to feel out of my depth. But she was busy selling bubble gum to a couple of eight-year-old toughies.

"Does he like the countryside?" I said, showing her a nice scene of fields and trees, with a thatched cottage in the foreground. She started hunting around in her handbag for her glasses. She'd forgotten the card she was holding. It fluttered to the ground. I picked it up.

"That's right," she said. "Drop everything on the floor. You need to be a bit more careful."

I decided to be ruthless.

"That's a nice card you've chosen," I said, putting the one I'd picked out in her hands. "Is it for anyone special?"

"Yes, it's for my brother," she said, suddenly all smiles.

"That's nice," I said, leading her up to the cash register. "It's his birthday, is it?"

"Yes." She leaned forward confidentially. "You'll never guess how old he is."

"No," I said. "I'm sure I wouldn't."

"Eighty-one!" she said triumphantly as I took a coin out of the open purse she held out toward me and put the change back into it. It's a good thing I'm honest. I could have helped myself to her old-age pension and she'd never have known the difference.

I got the giggles then. I had to turn away so that she wouldn't see. But when she'd gotten herself out of the shop, Mrs. Chapman turned on me.

"That's enough," she said sharply. I'd never heard her speak like that before. "I won't have you laughing at Miss Baggs, poor old lady. She used to be a music teacher. Highly respected. Spent years and years teaching snotty kids to play the piano. It's not her fault her memory's slipped a bit. She's a fine old lady. So don't let me catch you laughing at her again, mind."

I felt bad for a few minutes, but the shop was full, and by the time we'd served everyone, Mrs. Chapman was smiling and good-humored again. She was like that, Mrs. Chapman was. She never stayed cross for more than a minute at a time. And another thing I liked about her was that she had a lot of respect for people, even for old dears like Miss Baggs, who, say what you like, is as nutty as a fruitcake. Now that I come to think about it, she even had respect for Ben. By the middle of the after-noon my feet were like a couple of minced hamburgers. I'd worn these lovely shoes with red clip-on bows and high heels that I'd bought cheap on sale. They were a bit pinched around the toes, but I usually wore them when I was out because they looked so nice, and I suppose you have to suffer a bit for the sake of beauty. But after a few hours, my toes were killing me. I kicked the shoes off when I was behind the counter, but I could never spend long enough there for them to recover, because Mrs. Chapman kept saying, "Fetch me down another box of balloons from the top shelf, will you, Anna?" or "Pop out to the front and tidy up the magazine rack. It looks as if a bomb's hit it."

I could see why she needed an assistant. I don't know how she'd managed so long on her own. To reach the top shelves, she had to stand on a little stepladder, and I thought she'd wobble off more than once, she was so big and sort of stiff in her legs, and the steps were wobbly. But that made it all the nicer working for her. I knew I was being really useful, really earning my money.

I was beginning to feel that I'd been there forever, and could run the shop single-handed, when I had a shock. A posh woman in a fur coat and one of those expensive Hermès scarves with horses' heads and hooves and saddles all over it came up to the counter and bought a whole fistful of expensive magazines, like *Vogue* and *Harper's* and *Interiors.* I had never imagined that people, ordinary people I mean, actually bought that kind of thing. I'd only seen them in the dentist's waiting room. Anyway, this woman had such a high-class accent, I could hardly understand a word she said, and she had a sort of haughty way of looking at you down her long, powdered nose. I was idly watching her as she went down the shop on the way out, and she stopped at the pen rack and then, cool as a cucumber, she lifted a ballpoint out of the rack, slipped it into her pocket, and walked out, bold as brass.

I couldn't believe my eyes. I was sort of frozen with shock. I knew I should have run after her and told her to put it back, but her superior manner had made me kind of freeze up.

"Mrs. Chapman, that woman—the pen," I said incoherently.

"What's the matter, love?" said Mrs. Chapman, bending down with a creaking noise to rub the corn on her foot.

"That woman in the fur coat, she stole a ballpoint pen. I saw her. She just lifted it out of the rack and put it in her pocket."

To my surprise, Mrs. Chapman laughed.

"Oh, that must have been Mrs. Thompson," she said. "She's a shocker. Got a reputation for it. She only does it when her husband's at home. He works out in the Middle East somewhere. Makes pots of money, he does, and when he comes home, he gives her the devil. She goes a bit crazy. You'd never think she was a thief, dressed up to the nines like she is and all. She got arrested once. Mr. Featherstone, around the corner in the grocer's, he caught her red-handed with some fancy cookies. He doesn't hold with shoplifting. It makes him see red. So he wouldn't take an apology or anything, and he called the police. She had to go to court and go on trial and everything. Got off with a fine, though. Didn't have to do time, like most people. She was nice about it afterward. She came around and apologized to all the shopkeepers. Half of us had no idea what she'd been up to. She said she didn't know what came over her, and would I keep an eye on her and chalk up anything else she pinched on her newspaper bill. I'll say one thing for her, she never takes anything worth more than a dollar. And she gives me a whacking great Christmas box. More than makes up for the stuff she gets away with, I'm sure. What kind of pen was it, now? Fancy or plain?"

You certainly see a slice of life in a newsdealer's. I'd never have thought it. I'd never have imagined that someone like Mrs. Thompson, so grand and rich and respectable-looking, would be a thief.

I felt great that evening, going home with money in my pocket. It was a landmark in my life. I would have skipped down the road if I'd been a few years younger and my feet hadn't been killing me. I could imagine myself in a few years' time, being independent and on my own, leading my own life, earning my own money. I made great plans for saving up and opening a bank account and getting one of those stunning all-in-one radio-cassette players. But then I passed the bakery. That bakery's been there ever since I can remember. It calls itself a continental pâtisserie, but there's nothing foreign about the doughnuts and apple slices and cream horns that load the shelves and make you stop every time you pass the window. Every day they display a big cake, as a sort of centerpiece. When I was little, it was my dream that one day I'd march in and point to the window and say, very coolly, "I'll have the big one, please, in the middle."

That day the center cake was a chocolate one with whipped cream piped around the top, decorated with flaky almonds. I don't honestly know what came over me. A sort of rush of blood to the head, I suppose, or rather, to the heels, because they seemed to turn of their own accord and walk into the shop, and before I knew what had happened, I was back outside again with a large box in my hands. I felt like a bit of a fool then. There was too much for the five of us, even though Dad was at home for once, because Mom usually did a stir-fry on Saturday nights, which didn't leave any room for dessert. But so what? I knew Ben would love it. I could just picture him smearing it all over his face and then licking his fingers with a sort of astonished look in his eyes, as if he'd made a fantastic new discovery. And any-way, I felt like celebrating. I wanted them all to realize that I'd stepped a bit further on in my life.

It's surprising how quickly new things become routine. After only a few Saturdays at Mrs. Chapman's I felt I'd worked there for years. It was tiring at first. I had to think all the time about where to find things and about how much change to give, and I always had to look at the prices on every item instead of just ringing them up on the cash register, like Mrs. Chapman could. The first couple of weeks I went home exhausted and flopped into bed early on Saturday night, when Miranda was just be-ginning her nightly round, and slept in most of Sunday morning, testing my legs gingerly under the blankets whenever I half woke up, to see how stiff they were. At least after that first Saturday I'd learned my lesson about shoes. I wore my oldest, flattest, and most comfortable and couldn't have cared less how I looked.

Once I got used to it, though, I could have done the job with my eyes shut. Mrs. Chapman was lovely to work for. I did my best for her because I liked her so much, and I could see she really needed the help, but she was easygoing and appreciated anything I did that she hadn't asked me to do. I took quite a pride in the shop, as if it were my own, and I liked sorting out little corners for her that had lain undisturbed for years. I stopped telling Mom about it after she wanted to know why I couldn't do the same in my bedroom, but it wasn't the same at all. She couldn't see that. Mrs. Chapman gave me a bonus, sometimes, if I did something extra, like mucking out the mess under the counter or cleaning out the window and putting the display back properly. Perhaps if Mom had learned about bonuses, things might have been different at home.

It was the second Saturday in November when the phone in the back room suddenly rang. Mrs. Chapman was unpacking a load of early Christmas cards in there, so she answered it. I heard her say, "Oh yes, hello, Mrs. Peacock." And then there was a silence while Mom was obviously speaking at the other end. And then Mrs. Chapman said, "That's all right. I quite understand. Do you want to speak to her yourself, or shall I give her the message?" Then there was another long pause, and she said, "Don't worry, we're quiet in here today. She'll be with you in a few minutes."

"Ben," I thought. "Something's happened." But Mrs. Chapman didn't look upset or anything as she maneuvered her way through the small space between the stacks of newspapers that stood in the doorway of the back room.

"That was your mom," she said. "You'll have to run

along home. She's got to take Ben down for his appointment at the hospital, and your sister's come down with something. Temperature's way up, and she's feeling very sick. Your mom wants you to look after her."

She must have seen the face I pulled, because she gave one of her wheezy chuckles.

"Price of popularity, dear," she said. "Everyone seems to want you today."

Ten

KATY HAD THE FLU. AT LEAST, THAT'S WHAT MOM CALLED IT.
The doctor said it was a virus. He always says that. It
doesn't matter if you've gone blue with green spots and
your head's bursting and your cough is like Krakatoa
erupting, you've still only got a virus, and all he can do is
tell you to keep warm and drink plenty of fluid. I prefer
illnesses with proper names, like chicken pox or mumps.
At least you know then what you're in for.

I got it next. I had a temperature and I felt rotten for
a day or two, but I wasn't as bad as Katy. I only spent a
day in bed and then I mooned around downstairs in the
living room mainly, trying to summon up the energy to
finish my tapestry kit of a couple of ponies that Aunty
Janice had given me for my birthday. Aunty Janice didn't
realize, but I wasn't that keen on ponies. She'd been mad
about them at my age, so she expected me to be too. It
was too late to explain to her. She'd given me too many
horsy presents already. Anyway, I'd done the interesting
bits, and there were only acres of boring background left,
so I couldn't be bothered to do any more. I just lay on the

sofa reading a novel and minding Ben while Mom got on with the housework upstairs.

We've got a bookcase in our living room. It's got paperbacks on the top shelf, the Bible, Shakespeare, and dictionaries on the middle shelf, as well as a couple of ornaments, and some big, heavy books on the bottom, things like *The Country Diary of an Edwardian Lady* and *The Vogue Book of Fashion,* which Granny picks up cheap in bookstores and gives Mom for her birthday. Most of the big books have brightly colored covers and are shiny and eye-catching. I suppose that's why Ben could never leave them alone.

He'd learned how to move around by himself at long last, or at least to sort of roll himself along the floor. I suppose he'd have found his big head too hard to control if he'd tried to get about on his hands and knees. It was difficult to see exactly how he did it, but one moment he'd be chewing the edge of the curtain and the next moment he'd be over on the other side of the room, half inside the cupboard. Most children of his age, of course, would have been walking for a long time by now, but he could get around surprisingly fast, especially on the vinyl floor in the kitchen. Carpet slowed him down a bit. Surface tension or something, I suppose.

Anyway, that morning I was so busy reading my novel, I'd forgotten about Ben. I'd gotten to the bit where the miner's daughter had run away to London on the stagecoach and was roaming the streets in search of honest lodging, a prey to the lust and depravity of dissolute aristocrats and heartless highwaymen. I love historical novels. You can daydream better. Everything seems more dramatic and beautiful and highly colored, like in the theater.

I was jerked out of my book by a sudden crash. Ben had pulled half the books out of the bottom shelf.

"No!" I said loudly.

He jumped, startled, then looked around at me. His chin wobbled, and I thought he was going to cry, but then a sort of interested, curious look flitted across his face. His hand reached out again to the next book.

"No, Ben," I said. "Naughty. Stop it."

His eyes danced, and a grin, a purely mischievous, wicked grin spread over his face, and he rolled down the bookshelf a bit further and reached up, looking around at me, waiting for me to say no.

"No, Ben," I said, trying not to smile. "No!"

He stopped, put his hands over his eyes, and peeped at me through his fingers, chuckling with pleasure. Whatever else he hadn't got, Ben certainly had a sense of humor.

I knew that once he'd started, he'd go on playing his little game for hours, and I didn't feel up to responding to him, so I tidied up the bookshelf, got him a rusk from the kitchen, and pushed some chairs in front of the bookshelves so that he couldn't get at them again. He settled down quickly, sucking on his rusk and pushing his fluffy rabbit in and out of the wastepaper basket, and I went back to my book. If only I'd known, if only I'd realized, I'd have played with him all day, as long as he wanted, as long as he could.

I slept that afternoon, and when I woke up, I heard Ben whimpering. He went on and on, and I couldn't hear

Mom. I thought she might have popped out for a minute, so I went to see what the matter was. Mom was there. She was sitting in her favorite armchair with Ben on her knee, trying to give him a drink. He looked hot and flushed and kept pushing the cup away.

"He's got it," Mom said. "I knew he would. The doctor says to keep him warm and give him plenty to drink. More bad nights, I suppose. Pity your father's always away at exactly the wrong moment."

Ben was bad in the evening. He tossed about and moaned, and his temperature was way up. I didn't take much notice. He'd been this bad before. Katy had seemed much worse the first night she'd had it, and two days later she was bouncing around again, dressing herself up in Mom's old clothes and yelling, "Look! *Look* at me, Anna! Don't you think I'm like Princess Di?"

Mom gave Ben some children's aspirin in the end, and he quieted down a bit. Then she went to get his crib ready and gave him to me to hold, and I sang to him. He always loved singing. He knew "The Teddy Bears' Picnic" and "Hark! the Herald Angels" and "Happy Birthday to You." He could even beat time perfectly. I rocked him gently while I sang, and the beating slowly stopped, and his head fell back on my shoulder. He was asleep. Mom came then and took him out of my arms and up to his little bed, all soft and fleecy and baby-warm.

I think it was Ben's bedroom door banging shut that roused me, without really waking me up. I half heard Mom's feet pattering down the stairs and the buttons on the telephone clicking as she pressed the numbers. Then her voice, high and desperately afraid, came floating into my mind and merged with a dream of hospitals and a memory of Ben's birth.

"Dr. Randall? It's Mrs. Peacock here. I'm sorry to call you in the night, but it's Ben. He's not breathing right, and I can't rouse him. Please, oh can you . . . I'm so worried. . . . No, my husband's away at the moment. I'm on my own. Oh thank you, Dr. Randall. Fifteen minutes, you said?"

The receiver clicked down again, and she ran back upstairs and into Ben's room. I slipped back again into a deep sleep, as reality and the dream melted into nothingness.

It was probably the cough mixture Mom had given me that knocked me out completely that night. I didn't hear the doctor coming or the sound of him working over Ben's crib or Mom's frantic telephone calls to the hotel up north where Dad was staying or her first expressions of grief. I knew nothing till six o'clock in the morning, when she crept into my room and lay down beside me on my bed and burst into a storm of tears.

She didn't have to tell me what she was crying for. I had woken with a lead weight pressing down on my heart. I knew for sure that Ben was dead, as if God himself had told me. I couldn't cry. I lay there, rigid and dry-eyed, frozen with shock. I couldn't remember his name. I couldn't remember what he looked like. I wondered who this strange woman was who had come into my room and was lying on my bed. One word hammered away in my mind, blocking out everything else: "No! No! No!"

A sound made me look up. Katy stood in the door, her eyes wide, her mouth trembling.

"What is it?" she said. "Why's Mom crying?"

Mom sat up then and put her arms out. Katy went into them. She was crying in sympathy before she'd even heard what had happened.

"Ben's been very ill," Mom said.

A wild, insane joy surged through me. Had I misunderstood? Was there still hope? Katy waited, passively, to be told more. I waited, my heart in my mouth, to hear what I already knew.

"He's gone," said Mom. "He's passed away in the night."

"What do you mean?" said Katy. There was no point in trying to break it gently. Katy had to have everything spelled out to her, in black and white. I heard my own voice, sounding dry and harsh.

"She means he's dead," I said.

Katy burst at once into loud, easy sobs. She sat on Mom's knee and tried idiotically to comfort her.

"You've still got me," she said. "And Anna," she added as an afterthought. "Don't cry, Mom. I can't bear it. Please don't cry."

The doorbell rang. Mom lifted her head.

"That must be the nurse," she said. "Stay in here, you two. I'll go. Please stay in here. Anna, make sure Katy . . ." I nodded at her, and she left the room.

Katy went on sobbing for a while, but with less and less conviction. I could see she thought that crying was the correct thing to do, but I knew she was feeling excited as much as anything and full of curiosity.

"Why aren't you crying, Anna?" she said at last. "Don't you care?"

I took no notice. It wasn't worth bothering to answer. Ben had never been hers in the way he'd been mine. Anyway, I couldn't have spoken to anyone just then. I heard the tap running in the bathroom and a firm tread in the hall outside and a soothing, unfamiliar female voice. And then at last the sound of someone going down the stairs, and Mom came into my room.

"Come down, now," she said, "and eat your breakfast. Dad should be here soon."

Breakfast was a disgusting idea. The thought of food revolted me. But it was the next thing to do. You get up, you get dressed, then you have your breakfast. Even when there's a death in the house, that's what you do. If you stop doing that, life stops altogether. I managed to drink a cup of tea and pretended to have some toast. Katy ate a full bowl of cornflakes and asked for more. I had to keep telling myself that she was only ten.

Mom went to the telephone then, and I heard her speak to Granny, and then she went to her room and I went to mine. The house was uncannily still and quiet.

"This is what it's going to be like," I thought. "We'll miss the sound of him first."

I opened my door and went quietly along to Ben's room and slipped inside. The curtains had been drawn, and there was only a dim light coming into the room.

The nurse had moved the crib. It was in the wrong place, alone, in the middle of the room, where he couldn't see the pigeons, which were already pecking on the windowsill.

"I'll put it right for you," I whispered, and I pushed it back into place. Then I looked at him.

He was the same. He was himself, asleep. The bed-clothes were unnaturally tidy, that was all. One hand lay outside the coverlet, the little fingers curled up, relaxed. The nurse had brushed his hair, and his curls lay smooth as cream silk against his big, blue-veined head.

"Respiratory failure," Mom had said on the phone to Granny. I'd been afraid that he would look anguished, choking for breath, in pain, but he didn't. Just restful and quiet and happy.

My foot kicked against something soft. It was his fluffy rabbit. I picked it up and tucked it down beside him.

"There you are," I said. "There's rabbit."

My hand brushed against his face. It was cold, quite cold. I knew then. I couldn't pretend anymore that he would wake up in a minute and put out his arms, asking to be lifted. That was the moment when I believed that he was dead. But I knew, even then, that he was still with me, still near, still loving me. His spirit hadn't quite gone away. It lingered on, like a perfume when its wearer has just left the room.

I knelt down then, on the floor beside the crib and stroked his hand gently, because I was afraid I might disturb him. I talked to him. I told him things. I told him what had happened when I'd first seen him and how I'd loved him right away. I told him that he was the best kind of brother and that I'd never wanted him to be different. I told him I'd go on loving him forever, as long as I lived. I told him he'd be all right.

And then I kissed him, to say good-bye, and the frozen lump in my chest started to melt, and I ran out of his room and flung myself down on my bed. That's where Dad came to me, later. And when I saw him, I found at last that I could cry, and I couldn't stop, and we cried together until there were no tears left.

Eleven

I DON'T KNOW IF YOU'VE EVER BEEN TO A FUNERAL. IF YOU haven't, you probably think they're morbid and creepy. But if you've been to the funeral of someone you loved, you probably found, like I did, that it was a help. It was like having a nurse wash a nasty wound and put a plaster on it. You dread her touching it, and it hurts a lot at the time, but it's better afterward.

It was the days before the funeral that were so horrible. We lived in a peculiar limbo, with cards and letters arriving and Mom and Dad always on the telephone, and all the time I was thinking about Ben lying in the undertaker's chapel a couple of miles away.

Then there was school. Dad phoned Mrs. Gordon, and she told the class, so I didn't actually have to break the news, but I had to face everyone's sympathy. I could see that they were embarrassed and didn't know what to say. They either treated me like an invalid, too delicate to bear the slightest loud noise or sudden movement, and talked to me in hushed tones, being hideously tactful, or they avoided me altogether. I saw Sandra actually turn and double back down the corridor that ran alongside the gym when she saw me at the other end. She was great at battering a hockey ball through a solid line of hearty defenders, but give her a human problem and she went to pieces. I expected Miranda to understand, but she'd gone and caught the virus. She sent me a note, which made me cry, and I could see she felt miserable about Ben. She'd loved him a lot. But it was Debbie, unpredictable, self-controlled Debbie, who really surprised me.

"There's no point in pretending I know how you feel," she said bluntly as we sat on the radiator by the window, waiting for Mrs. Hamilton to turn up for English, "because nothing so awful has ever happened to me. I don't even know what to say or whether you want to talk about it. Well? Do you want to?"

It was lovely to be with someone straightforward. Debbie didn't deal in evasions. She bludgeoned straight through to the heart of the matter, brushing aside obstacles with a swish of her beautiful hair, and she couldn't understand why other people didn't do the same.

"Tell me what happened," she said. "Were you with him all the time? Did he cry a lot? Did it hurt?"

I began to talk then, answering her hesitantly at first and then going on and on, until I was pouring everything out, breaking off to borrow her tissues when I cried, going over his last day and the dreadful morning when it had happened. I hardly noticed that the rest of the class had fallen silent and that they'd gathered around to listen. I didn't mind. I wanted to talk and talk. I found myself repeating things over and over again.

"Why?" I kept saying. "Why did he have to be born like that? It's so unfair. Why did he have to die? What was God thinking about, making a child suffer like that? Where was God when he died?"

My questions hung in the air. Not even Debbie tried to answer. I could see prissy Lucy screwing up her face and trying to fish out a quote from the Bible to throw at me. She's very religious and thinks she knows all the answers. But then Mrs. Hamilton's rich, deep voice suddenly broke in. She must have been standing at the back of the group listening.

"Even such is Time, that takes in trust
Our youth, our joys, our all we have,
And pays us but with earth and dust."

Trust her to have a poem ready on the tip of her tongue.

"Come on, everyone," she said. "Get back to your places. Anna's asked some very important questions, and we're going to discuss them."

I was furious with her. I felt she was taking my feelings away from me and exploiting them for her silly English lesson. But it didn't work out like that. It was really good. If Mrs. Hamilton never makes it as an actress, she'll still have a great future on TV doing one of those discussion shows where they invite people who wildly disagree with each other and someone has to sit in the middle and sort of conduct it all.

After that, school was all right. It didn't exactly get back to normal, but the ice was broken. It was much harder at home. Mom was up and down like a seesaw, sometimes talking nonstop to whoever would listen to her in a way that was quite unlike her and then clamming up and going to her bedroom and not answering even the simplest questions. The neighbors weren't much help. They were mostly like the girls had been at school, too embarrassed to say anything and keeping out of our way. Mrs. Russell from next door tried to be nice. She brought in little presents, a bunch of flowers or a tin of homemade flapjacks. It wasn't the presents so much as the feeling that she was thinking of us in a kind way. But then she messed it up by saying to Mom, "You'll soon get over it. It's a blessed release, really, isn't it?"

Mom was really mad with her. She'd said to Granny herself, I'd heard her, that at least Ben had been released from a lot of suffering, but she didn't like anyone else saying it. And she knew, we all knew, that we'd never get over it. You never get over some things. You just learn to live with them. Mrs. Russell made it even worse by going on and on about how she understood, because her husband had died last year, and she talked about it nonstop, and you couldn't help feeling that she was only coming around all the time because she was lonely and wanted us to sympathize with her. She'd get off the subject of Ben as soon as it came up and get back onto the subject of her Percy.

Katy didn't help. She veered from being moody and tearful to being horribly bright and cute and little-girly, trying to get everyone's attention. I didn't have any patience with her at all. But two days before the funeral I found her sitting in her wardrobe, where she often goes if she's upset, and she looked so still and woebegone that I felt sorry for her.

"What's the matter with you?" I said.

She said nothing, but held up a little china Bambi that Granny had given her when she was three. It was her dearest possession. She always said that if there was a fire and she only had time to grab one thing, she'd go for her Bambi.

"What's happened to it?" I said. "Have you broken it or something?"

She shook her head, so I sat down on the floor and waited. Katy always tells you things in the end. You just have to give her time. She's the sort who can never keep anything secret. Not like me. I often imagine I'm being tortured and that I'm not telling the names of my fellow revolutionaries. I know I'd be able to keep my trap shut. It's one of my greatest talents.

I got it out of Katy quite quickly. She was feeling awful because she'd never let Ben touch Bambi and he'd often wanted to. He used to point to it and whimper and she'd always snatched it out of reach and run off. Sometimes she'd even teased him with it to make him cry. But now she was so sorry and she felt so bad about it, and she wanted to give Bambi to Ben to take with him. I was shocked at that. It didn't seem decent to me. But then Katy started to cry, and once she started, she couldn't stop, and then Dad came in and asked what the fuss was all about. So I explained it, and he thought for a bit, and then to my surprise he took Katy's part. He said it was a very nice idea, and he would take her to the undertaker's that afternoon, and she could see Ben in the chapel there.

Dad has never been known to refuse Katy anything, at least not that I can think of. It's the worst thing about him. I don't know why I said I wanted to go too. I suppose it was because I was restless and thinking about Ben all the time and I felt drawn to him, as if there was a piece of elastic pulling me.

I hadn't realized that the coffin would be so small, lying there on a big table in the chapel of rest. It was white, with silver handles, and when Mr. Roberts, the undertaker, opened it and put back the lid, I saw that it was lined with white satin. I felt good about that. It was like a little crib, cozy and comfortable. I looked down at Ben, expecting him to be the same as when I'd seen him last, but he wasn't. He looked kind of pinched and waxen. But the real change was that now I could see he had gone. His spirit was no longer there, hovering like an invisible sweetness in the air. It had flown away. It was only his shell left in the box, as meaningless now as the chrysalis that the butterfly sloughs off. I was grateful to Katy. I was glad I'd seen him again. I put my arm around her as we looked down at him together. She snuggled into me. I'd hardly ever cuddled her, but I enjoyed it. I felt a rush of affection for her. She looked up at me.

"I'm the youngest now, aren't I, Anna?" she said. I realized then that it had been tough for Katy too. Ben had robbed her of her mother for more than two years of her childhood. He'd taken me away too. I'd had no time for her while he had been alive. I gave her shoulders a squeeze.

"Go on, then," I said. "Where's Bambi?"

She pulled it out from under her sweatshirt, gave it a

last kiss, stroked its glazed back, and put it down beside Ben.

"Do you think he knows?" she said.

"Yes, of course he does," I said, and the extraordinary thing was, I felt absolutely sure about it. "He knows, and he's really pleased, and it was a very nice thing to do."

The day of the funeral was bright and sunny. It was one of those days in early winter when everything is golden and glowing; and scarlet berries, huge spiders' webs, curled yellow leaves, and bulbous brown seed heads make sort of still-life pictures everywhere you look. It seemed all wrong to me. I'd imagined the funeral on a dark and gloomy day, with dripping trees and mist.

It started off badly. I wanted to wear something black, or at least as dark as possible. I chose my clothes carefully. Dad said most people didn't bother with mourning nowadays, but I wanted to wear it. It seemed right to me. But Mom went all funny about it. We had a stupid argument, and then she said, "You wear what you like, then, but I'm going to wear my red coat whatever you say. Ben liked the fur on the collar. He used to stroke it." And then she cried, and I realized I was being tactless and interfering, so I shut up. I thought of offering to lend her my red scarf to go with it, just to show her that I was sorry, but something told me that it wouldn't be a good idea.

The church was full of flowers. It was strangely beautiful, like at a wedding. There were quite a lot of people there, some old friends of Mom's and Dad's and people who lived in our street. Mrs. Russell was as near the front as she could get without sitting in the seats reserved for the family. She honestly looked as if she was enjoying herself.

Mr. Henderson seemed different when he came in. Sort of solemn, but powerful and in command too. I felt at last that here was someone who understood what was going on. It was like being in a strange new building and finding someone who's got the keys. Mr. Henderson has got keys. I don't mean to the church hall or anything, but keys to secrets about life that he knows how to unlock.

I don't remember everything that happened at the funeral. I just remember the little coffin, shining, bathed in sunlight, speckled in jewellike colors from the stained-glass window, heaped up with white and yellow flowers. And I remember that the words of the service rolled on majestically, like waves breaking on a beach, and I remember that I no longer wanted to curse and shout, "Where were you, God, the night Ben died?" I felt that somewhere there was a meaning and that one day I would know what it was, and that I was loved and I had to trust that love and let Ben go away into its arms, and that one day I would go out into it too.

At the end of the service there was a silence, and when the minister looked around at us all, and he smiled and said with a kind of power and confidence in his voice, " 'Blessed are the pure in heart, for they shall see God.' "

I could tell it was a quote from somewhere. The Bible, I suppose. But it described Ben exactly. Pure in heart, that was Ben. It made Mom start crying again, and she clutched Dad's arm, but I found myself nodding, and Katy looked up at me, and she smiled, and I know she felt like I did, that Ben was safe with God.

Twelve

I can't remember much about the weeks after Ben's funeral. I suppose, being November, that it was wet, cold and gloomy. But I didn't seem to notice the weather, or anything else happening outside myself either. I had this dull, heavy pain that sat on my chest like a weight, and nothing else mattered.

The strange thing was that life seemed to go on quite normally at school. I didn't know how to explain to anyone that to me things had changed completely, and changed forever. I felt different from all the others, as if I was speaking a new language or seeing through different glasses, or as if I'd gone into another dimension of life or something.

After a couple of weeks everyone at school seemed to think that it was all over and that I must have gotten over Ben by this time, and they stopped being embarrassed or especially nice or anything. In a way, that was a help. I had to go back to doing the same old things, like playing hockey and getting French homework in on time and worrying about my low marks in math. But all the time, while I was pretending to be just the same as everyone else, I carried this churned-up, desperate misery inside me.

Sometimes it lifted for a few moments. Occasionally, when I woke up in the morning, I felt quite ordinary again, and I'd think, "That's nice. I haven't felt like this in ages. Why not?", and then I'd remember, and it would be as if the ton of concrete that was pressing down on my chest had gotten even heavier. Even in the daytime I had moments when I forgot about Ben. I'd be reading *Pride and Prejudice* or having an argument about abortion or something, and then I'd suddenly realize I hadn't thought about him for half an hour.

At first, when that happened, I felt guilty, as if I'd betrayed him, and I'd whisper to myself, "I'm sorry. I haven't forgotten. I'll never forget." But then, slowly, the time when I wasn't thinking about him got longer and the times when I was got shorter. And when I did think about him, it got harder and harder to remember what he was really like or to conjure up the sound of his voice or the smell of his freshly washed hair.

At least things were better at home. Dad had started his new job now. He had to leave the house early every day and he got home quite late, but the main thing was that he didn't have to keep going away all the time. And Mom had stopped sniping at him, too. In fact, they'd become so lovey-dovey again all of a sudden that there didn't seem much room for anyone else.

Don't get me wrong. I hadn't exactly liked them going off each other. I mean, the last thing I wanted was a broken home, on top of everything else. It was just that they seemed as if they didn't need anyone except each other. When Dad had been away, Mom had gotten into the habit of talking to me a bit about how she felt about things, but she didn't do it anymore. Maybe she thought it would just make me feel worse or something. Even when I knew she was miserable, she'd put on a show and pretend to cheer up when I was around. It was only with Dad that she let her hair down, and he was the same with her. Nobody seemed to need me, not even Katy, much. Anyway, Katy doesn't really count as a person when it comes to that sort of thing. She's just a child.

People outside the family were just as bad. When anyone came to the house, they always seemed to think it was worst for Mom. And I suppose it was, in a way, but nobody seemed to think it was particularly sad for me. Maybe sisters don't usually love brothers the way I loved Ben. Maybe.

Not that many people came to the house after the first week or two. Mr. Henderson called a few times, and some people came from the day care center Ben had started going to. But Mrs. Russell was still in and out all the time, even though we were all fed up with her. Only two days after the funeral she marched in through the back door into the kitchen and said to Mom, "What are you going to do with all his things, then, his clothes and his crib and all?"

Mom went red and spoke quite sharply. "We'll be making arrangements, thank you."

And Mrs. Russell said, "Only there's my Sharon, and she's expecting her third after Christmas, and I know she could do with some new stuff, cheap."

LOVING BEN

I sat there with my hands clenched, hoping that
Mrs. Russell would drop dead or that lightning would
strike the house or that anything would happen to stop
Mom from giving Ben's precious things to Mrs. Russell's
nasty Sharon and Sharon's nasty babies, who always
have runny noses and look spoiled and whiny. But I
needn't have worried.

"I'll let you know if there's anything suitable,"
Mom said, and pressed her lips closely together, so that I
could see she was annoyed. But after that, every time I
saw Mrs. Russell, I thought of her trying to get her hands
on Ben's things and it made me boil. I didn't want anyone to touch them. They were sacred.

I hadn't been in Ben's room much since the funeral. I
suppose Mom went in to clean as usual, because there
was never any dust or anything in there. I don't know
why, but I just didn't feel like going in. I didn't want to. I
didn't even like it if the door was left open, so that I
could see in when I went past to my own room. The
empty crib and the mobile hanging from the light and
the soft toys lined up on the chest of drawers gave me a
sort of painful jolt, and I couldn't help thinking of the
clothes in the drawers, still neatly folded up, ready to be
used, just as they had been the day he died. The room
had that sad, packaged-up feel about it, like when people
are just about to move away.

It was the moth that got things moving. I heard Dad
swatting it on the stairs.

"That's the second one this week," he said, coming
into the living room, where I was supposed to be doing
my homework and Mom was drying Katy's hair.

"They'll be into everything if we don't watch out. You should have seen Bill's father's coat when the moths got at it after it had been put away in a cupboard for six months."

"What do you mean?" said Katy, looking alarmed. "Do you mean they eat clothes? What about my new disco pants?"

That's typical Katy. Obsessed with clothes. I can't think where she gets it from. Mom's not a bit like that, and neither am I.

"Don't be silly," said Mom, sort of absentmindedly. "Nobody's going to eat your disco pants. They only go for stuff that's not often used," and I saw that she was looking steadily at Dad.

"We'll have to go through it all sometime, love," said Dad gently. "It can't just sit there forever. I think the moment's come, don't you?"

Mom stood perfectly still, the hairbrush raised in one hand, the hair dryer in the other poised over Katy's head.

"Ow!" said Katy, twisting around as the heat got too much for her scalp.

Mom pushed the hair dryer and the brush into my hands.

"You finish her off, Anna," she said, and she followed Dad out of the room and up the stairs.

It was too much. It was like all the other things they'd done over the past few weeks. They were pushing me out. Shutting me off, as usual. Treating me as if I didn't exist. I flung the brush down and thrust the hair dryer at Katy.

"You can do your own hair for a change," I said, "and your eyebrows, too, if you like," and I stormed off up the stairs to Ben's room and threw the door open.

"What about me?" I burst out. "It's my business just as much as yours. Why can't I . . . ?" and then I saw Mom and shut up. She was sitting on the floor holding up the green dungarees Ben had worn all last summer, and tears were running down her cheeks.

"Do you remember," she said, looking at Dad, "the day we went to the fair and some idiot gave him cotton candy?"

"What are you doing with them?" I said, not feeling angry anymore, but hurt instead. "Why can't I help too?"

"You can," said Dad. "Sit down."

It sounds dumb to say this, but we were happy that evening, in a funny sort of way. It was almost a relief to take out the little vests and jackets and pajamas and touch them again. They'd been lurking all these weeks like work that you know you've got to do but you can't get around to doing it. Unfinished business. It was painful, but nice too, like touching a scar when it hasn't completely healed.

We sorted everything into piles, and we kept stopping to remember things. Sometimes we even laughed, in a watery sort of way. Sometimes we cried a bit. At least Mom did, especially when she found the hat she'd made for Ben to wear. It was so big and looked so strange and unbabyish beside all the other, normal baby clothes.

"He only wore it once," she said, and she put it to one side, by itself.

"What are we going to do with them all?" I asked when the drawers were empty. I suddenly realized that we couldn't just put them back in the cupboard and leave them there.

"Not the trash can," said Mom, firmly.

"Not Sharon, either," I said, just as firmly.

"I think," said Dad, looking at Mom with a sort of watchful expression on his face, as if he thought she might explode or something, "that we ought to take them down to the Salvation Army shop."

I opened my mouth to say no, but then I shut it again. I saw a sudden picture in my mind's eye of a little ragged kid with one of those big potbellies, holding out his hand for one of Ben's nice fluffy things to put on, and I liked it.

"Can't we keep one or two?" I said, and Dad looked relieved.

"Good idea," he said, but he was still looking at Mom.

She reached out without a word and pulled a couple of things out of the piles—a little red cardigan and a pair of furry slippers and an embroidered bib. But when Dad looked at me and waited for me to take something, I found I couldn't. I couldn't bear to touch the clothes again. They were cold and lifeless. I suddenly wanted them to go, to be out of the house.

"It's all right," I said, "I can always look at Mom's pile if I want to," and I got up and left them to it. Dad had already started packing things into plastic bags, and I didn't feel like helping.

He must have taken them down to the Salvation

Army shop while I was at school the next day, because when I came home, Ben's room was empty. Even the crib had gone. There was just the old chest of drawers in there and the spare bed, which someone had moved in from Katy's room.

Thirteen

———

SPRING CAME AT LAST. IT WAS ALMOST A SURPRISE. I'D GOT to feeling that winter and the darkness and cold would last forever. But when it came, it sort of came in my mind, too.

I was still working at Mrs. Chapman's on Saturdays. It was great, actually. She wasn't like other people, who mostly shied away from the subject of Ben as if it was indecent to talk about him or something. She often mentioned him, in a casual, ordinary way, as if he was still alive. It made me feel better, I don't know why.

I'd gotten used to the work in the shop. I didn't have to think about it much anymore. I knew where everything was, and I knew a lot of the customers too. Quite often there were gaps when no one came in, even though Saturday morning was one of the busiest times of the week, and when I wasn't in the middle of dusting shelves or unpacking a new delivery of pencil sharpeners, I had time to daydream. Mrs. Chapman laughed at me and said my head was so high up in the air I'd never keep my feet on the ground, but she didn't mean to be nasty.

One morning I was in a particularly dreamy mood. I'd seen a beautiful film on TV the night before, and it had filled me full of a sort of mellow yearning. A dark-haired woman was buying a newspaper up at the counter, waiting for Mrs. Chapman to finish serving someone else and take her money. I went down to the front of the shop to restock the rack of newspapers that hung just outside the doorway. When I turned back and went around the central island to check on the stationery, I was jerked out of my daydream.

A stroller was parked right up next to the freezer, where the ice creams were kept. The little girl, sitting quietly in it, was handicapped. She had round plastic glasses on, which were barely held up by her small button nose. Her head was a slightly unusual shape, and her eyes had that Oriental look, pulled up at the edges. Her tongue was sticking out a bit, and a line of dribble ran down her chin. It wasn't the little girl who gave me the shock, though. It was the position in which her mother had left the stroller. It was exactly where I had left Ben, that morning when Miranda had seen him for the first time. I'd chosen the spot because I'd thought it was out of sight. I knew for sure, I was absolutely certain, that this little girl's mother had left her here for exactly the same reason. Memories came flooding back. My heart turned over.

"Ben," I thought. "Oh, Ben."

The little girl looked up at me. Most people wouldn't have called her pretty. They wouldn't have seen past the things that made her look different. But she looked lovely to me. The eyes behind her glasses were big and fringed with long black lashes. Her hair, black and straight, was tied in two bunches on each side of her head, and it looked as soft as feathers. It was hard to tell her age. I guessed she was about four. She smiled when she saw me looking at her, and leaning forward in her stroller, she flapped her hand in my direction and blew a big bubble out of her mouth. I heard footsteps coming down the shop and sensed that her mother was behind me, waiting for me to finish whatever I was doing and go back to the counter. Instead, I knelt down by the stroller and tickled the little girl under her ear.

"You're nice, aren't you?" I said. "What a beautiful smile you've got!"

She wriggled with pleasure, put one fat little hand over her mouth, then put it out toward me.

"Aren't you clever! You can blow kisses!" I said. "I bet they're all in love with you at home."

The woman behind me had made no move. I turned to look at her. She looked defensive and wary. She was watching me carefully. She didn't know what I was up to. She almost looked too old to be the little girl's mother. Her strong, dark hair was streaked with gray. She looked too kind of elegant, too, to have a young kid. She had on the kind of coat my Mom doesn't even dare look at in the shops, and she was wearing those really modern metal earrings. She smiled at me hurriedly, as though she wanted to get out of my way, squeezed past me to get behind the stroller, and moved toward the door of the shop.

"What's your little girl's name?" I asked. "She's a darling, isn't she?"

The woman looked at me in surprise. I could guess she wasn't used to people telling her that. Then she gave me a beaming smile. Her face changed completely.

"Jackie," she said, in a slightly foreign accent. "Her name's Jackie." She hesitated. "She's not quite . . . not quite right. She's got Down's syndrome." She rolled the r, but said the medical terms easily. It was obvious she'd said them many times before.

"She's not as handicapped as my brother was," I said.

"Your brother?" she said inquiringly. I knew I had caught her interest now.

"Yes," I said, "I had a brother who was, well, very handicapped. But he was . . ." To my embarrassment I heard my voice shaking. "He was lovely," I finished lamely.

She tactfully stopped looking at me, bent over Jackie, did up a button on her little coat, and caressed her cheek with the tips of her fingers. I didn't realize till afterward that she hadn't asked the usual question. Being foreign, perhaps she hadn't noticed that "was" in the past tense. Or perhaps she was just too tactful to ask.

"Good-bye," she said. "See you again, maybe."

"I hope so," I said. "Good-bye, Jackie. Be a good girl now," and I went to the shop door to watch them as they scurried down the street, until they had turned into the butcher's and were lost to view.

I saw Jackie and her mother quite often after that. They obviously liked coming into Mrs. Chapman's, like I used to with Ben. They felt her friendliness and kindly interest, so different from the averted eyes up at the supermarket. Mrs. Maynard (I learned her name because she put in an order for a foreign newspaper) didn't talk much at first. She wasn't a chatty kind of person. But Mrs. Chapman soon got her going. Mrs. Chapman would have coaxed a brick wall to talk to her if there'd been no one else around. You could tell Mrs. Maynard was lonely. She'd only just moved to this neighborhood, she said, and she was alone with Jackie most of the time. Her older child was nineteen and away at college. She never mentioned her husband, but she looked so mournful a lot of the time that I sort of assumed she was a widow. I listened with half an ear while the two of them were talking, but the rest of me was busy with Jackie.

Every time they came, Jackie and I had our little chat. I remembered what Ben had liked, and I guessed she'd like it too. Mrs. Maynard would push her up to the counter (she didn't hide her anymore) and I'd blow Jackie a kiss. She'd blow one back, then I'd kneel down and point to her shoes and say, "Nice shoes," or something and work slowly upward, saying, "What pretty socks," or "What a lovely dress," and things like that till I got to the ribbon in her hair. I must say, she was always beautifully turned out. Mrs. Maynard adored her. You could see that. And she was cute, Jackie was. If I missed out something, she'd grab my hand and make me touch it, so that I had to be sure to notice everything, in the right order. And when we'd finished our little panto-mime, I'd give her something out of one of the big jars Mrs. Chapman kept behind the counter, full of toffees and peppermint creams and hard candies wrapped in cel-lophane. Mrs. Chapman didn't mind. She only said that I had to square it with Mrs. Maynard first, because these days you never knew what kind of funny notions mothers might have about their child's diet.

"I can't see that a few sweets now and then could harm a kiddie," she said. "But then, I'm old-fashioned." I said nothing. You only had to look at Mrs. Chapman to see that she had a fondness for sweets herself, but I thought it was best to keep a tactful silence on any subject that was remotely connected with weight.

Jackie used to go wild with joy when she got her sweet. Lots of kids, when they get a treat, whine and plead for another before they've even got the wrapping off the first. You see some nasty little brats when you work in a shop like Mrs. Chapman's. It makes you wonder sometimes. I always used to think Mom was much too strict, but I'm glad now that she brought me up properly. There's nothing worse than a sniveling, spoiled child. Jackie wasn't a bit like that. She knew the art of enjoying things in a simple, wholehearted way without having half an eye to anything else that might be forthcoming.

When they were ready to go, I'd walk over to the door of the shop if there wasn't a line waiting to be served and wave bye-bye to Jackie. She couldn't say any words except "mumumum," which might have meant "Mom," I suppose, but she knew how to wave bye-bye all right.

"God's little clowns, they call those kids," said Mrs. Chapman, heaving a sentimental sigh. "You've got a lovely touch with her, Anna. Make a good Mom yourself one day."

I was sick of people saying things like that to me. Mrs. Chapman was like Mom. She said it because she thought it would encourage me, but it had the opposite effect. It reminded me of how I used to feel—that I was a flop, a failure, a nitwit, a Pea-brain, and that no boy had ever even sent me a Valentine's Day card (except one from Joe once, because Miranda had put him up to it, but that didn't count), let alone asked me out.

I'd given up all hope of seeing Tony again. He'd been a shadowy dream figure for so long that he was little more than a name and an impression to me now. I'd almost forgotten what he looked like. I'd sort of forgotten about Jeff too. I don't know why, but after Ben died, I hadn't gone to the youth club. I hadn't really meant to give it up, but I'd missed a couple of weeks, and then another, and then it seemed sort of embarrassing to go again. But in the back of my mind I had a feeling that sometime I'd go back, only next time I wouldn't be all shy and awkward. I'd be confident and relaxed.

On the outside, I suppose I was the same, but inside I knew I was changing. I wasn't the same twit who could be knocked out cold for six months just by seeing a boy at the tennis courts. I suppose, once you've thought so much about death, you feel you've got a stronger hold on life, in a funny sort of way. You feel more daring and that your time is precious. You don't want to waste it worrying about not being as good as everyone else. And that makes you look at other people more clearly too. Like I said, I felt as if I was seeing the world through a new kind of glasses.

Mrs. Maynard didn't come in the next Saturday. At

lunchtime I said to Mrs. Chapman, "No Jackie today, then?"

"No," she said. "They came in yesterday, though. Had a card to put in my window. She's looking for someone to look after Jackie for three weeks in the summer. Come to think of it, Anna, why don't you take her phone number? It would be just the job for you."

As soon as she said it I knew she was right. Dad had planned a vacation this year, but that would only be for two weeks at the end of the summer, and I'd given up on the idea of tennis coaching. I was getting sick of being taught all day long. I thought it might be nice to be in charge of someone else for a change. Looking after Jackie, I could earn some money and enjoy myself at the same time.

Suddenly I felt I had to get the job. And the card in the window was a threat. Suppose someone else had spotted it and phoned up Mrs. Maynard already? I watched in agony as a young mom with a toddler stopped outside and read through all the advertisements on the window. I willed the one about Jackie to drop off and disappear, but it didn't. If anything, it seemed to get bigger. It was practically luminous in my eyes. I saw the woman open her bag, take out a pencil, and start writing something down. I couldn't bear it any longer.

"Please, Mrs. Chapman," I said, "can I phone Mrs. Maynard now? I'm scared someone else'll get there first."

She laughed.

"Cat on hot bricks you've been the last ten minutes," she said. "So that's the problem, is it? Yes, go ahead, my love. I don't mind. Phone's still out the back, if it hasn't walked away."

I knew as soon as Mrs. Maynard picked up the receiver that I'd be all right. I'm often like that about phone calls. It must be my psychic sense again. At first, though, it seemed as if I'd gotten it wrong. She sounded rather stiff.

"Yes? What do you want?" she said, and her foreign accent sounded more obvious than ever over the phone.

"It's about your ad at the newsdealer's," I said, suddenly breathless with nerves.

"Yes?" she said, sounding even more guarded.

"It's me," I said stupidly. "You know me. I'm Anna. I'm the girl who works for Mrs. Chapman in the shop on Saturdays. I know Jackie. I often talk to her. You—"

She interrupted me. It was as if a cork had come out of a bottle. I had to hold the phone six inches away from my head like Mom does with Aunty Janice. It took me a while to untangle what she said, but the gist of it was that yes, she knew who I was, and yes, I was just the right person, and would I really do it, and she'd pay me properly, and I wouldn't believe how worried she'd been about leaving Jackie with a stranger, and she'd had a couple of funny calls after she'd put up her ad, and she'd gotten so nervous (only she pronounced it "nerrr-vous") she'd nearly decided not to take this course after all, but she wanted to so badly because she'd been on her own with Jackie for four years, because her husband had left her after Jackie was born, and she'd have to get back to work in the end, wouldn't she, and didn't I agree that the right way to start was to take a refresher course, because she'd been a bilingual secretary, Italian and English, but she'd never used word processors, and these days didn't I think it was pointless even to try for a job unless you did?

All I had to do was stand there and say, "Yes, no, yes, no," and worry about Mrs. Chapman's phone bill, but at long last she paused to breathe, and I asked when did she want me to start. That set her off again. Only now she went on about Jackie, and how affectionate she was, and how nice it was to have such a loving child, and how important it was to be patient and slow, and how I'd be the right person because I had such heart, because of my brother, and how safe she would feel with Jackie in such good hands.

I saw an opening then and quickly said that Mrs. Chapman was waiting for me, and she yelled her address at me two or three times, and I said I'd be in touch nearer the time.

"Told her your life story, then, did you?" said Mrs. Chapman dryly when I got back into the shop at last. I could see she was put out with me for being on the phone for so long. She's funny about the phone. She never uses it unless she has to, and when she does, she talks in a loud, high-pitched voice, in short, sharp sentences, as if she was using a code or something. But I'd been well trained by Dad. He's neurotic about the phone bill too. So I fished out fifty cents and put it in the till.

"You don't have to do that, love," said Mrs. Chapman, but I could tell she was mollified. And she didn't take it out again either.

It wasn't until I got home that evening and was sitting in front of the TV that I realized how excited I was. Dad was lovely about it.

"Earning your own living already," he said. "I'll be nice to you now, Pollyanna, so that you'll buy me a Porsche when you've made your first million."

Katy was jealous.

"Oh, you are lucky," she said. "It's not fair. You'll have lots more money than me, and you don't even like buying clothes."

Mom was guarded.

"It's a good idea," she said. "I'm sure you'll be a great help to Mrs. Maynard, but you'll have to be a bit less scatty in someone else's house. The mess in your bedroom . . . !"

But they'd all gotten it wrong. It wasn't the money I was after. It wasn't even the feeling of being out at work. I just wanted to be with a child again. A special child, who would need me. A child like Ben.

Fourteen

⎯⎯

THAT NIGHT I HAD A STRANGE DREAM. I WAS SUNBATHING IN a big park, near a lake, and there were lots of people out enjoying themselves. And all of a sudden a little hand caught at my leg, and I sat up. It was Ben.

He looked up at me and laughed and laughed, putting his head on one side in the adorable way he had. And I said, "Ben! Where have you been? Why did you leave us! Who's looking after you? Are you all right?"

Then Mrs. Maynard came up and said, "He came to me, you know, and he's quite happy. I didn't like to tell you. They wouldn't let me. They had reasons, I'm sure."

And then Ben rolled away very fast, toward the lake, and I ran after him, but the more I tried, the slower I got, and when I did reach him, he was slippery, as if his body was covered with oil, and I couldn't pick him up. He slithered into the water and sank, and I saw his face lying quite still, with ripples above gently distorting it. It was his dead face that I'd seen in his coffin.

I tried and tried to plunge in and get him out, but Mrs. Maynard stopped me, and we fought on the edge of the lake. My arms and legs were caught, held in her vise-like grip. And then she let me go, and said, "Look."

I looked down into the water, and Ben's eyes were open, and he was smiling at me, and it was his living face again. And he turned over like a little fish, so free and happy, without any of the awkwardness or jerkiness he'd had in real life, supple and strong, and he swam away, into the middle of the lake, and disappeared. I burst out crying and kept calling and calling to him to come back, but Mrs. Maynard turned me around, and there was Jackie, whimpering in her stroller. Mrs. Maynard said, "She's seen a little girl over there with an ice cream. Can you get her one, Anna?"

I woke up then, hot and sweating and all tangled up in my sheet, which had wound itself around my legs. I lay there for a long time, savoring the closeness to Ben, looking with my mind's eye at his face as it appeared in the dream. I'd often tried to remember what he looked like, but I could only see him as he appeared in photographs. In my dream he'd been absolutely real, himself, so close to me, but so horribly out of reach. I cried in earnest then, and it was as if he'd just died, the grief was so new. It twisted me all up inside, and I felt it would always be there, as fresh and as agonizing as on the day he was buried.

The funny thing was, though, that by the time I'd gotten up and had breakfast, the living image of Ben had faded again, and when Mom asked me what I was intending to take with me on vacation and would I like a new bathing suit because she'd seen some down on Main Street, I was nearly back to normal all of a sudden. It was as if a crack in a wall had appeared, and I'd been able to peep into another room, but the crack had been plastered over again, and there was no way I could open it up.

I'd told Mrs. Maynard that we'd be going away in the middle of August, and she planned to take her course at the beginning of the summer, so it was soon after the end of the term that I found myself on the doorstep of the apartments where she lived, ringing the front bell and waiting for the door buzzer to sound.

It's always a funny feeling going into someone's place for the first time. You see things so sharply. It's like I said, first impressions are the important ones. Mrs. Maynard's flat was small, but it was very neat and tidy. There were no odd chairs and cushions in random, dingy colors like there are in our house. There were no drooping, straggling houseplants that everyone forgets to water or shelves piled untidily with odd bits and pieces. There wasn't any mess. Everything had been neatly put away. One day, I thought, when I had my own place, it would be like this, all neat and tidy and properly looked after and uncluttered.

The best thing was that Jackie was so pleased to see me. She ran straight up to me, put her arms around my leg, and rested her head against my knee. It was the first time I'd seen her since my dream, and I felt quite choked up for a moment. I bent down and picked her up, and she hugged me and patted my hair. Then she struggled to be free, so I put her down and she tugged at my hand.

"She wants to show you her chair in the kitchen," said Mrs. Maynard, with the indulgent voice she always used when she talked about Jackie. "Go with her. We'll show you around the whole apartment so that you'll know where to find everything."

The tour didn't take long. There was the kitchen, the small living room with a shelf of toys all standing in a tidy line, the bathroom, and Jackie's room. She didn't actually show me her own bedroom, though I was dying to see it. She just opened the door a crack, giving me a glimpse of a peach-colored bedspread, and passed on. The last door she didn't open at all.

"This is my son's," she said. "He's away at college. I don't know if he comes this week. With boys you never know!"

It was hours before Mrs. Maynard had finished giving me my instructions. Jackie had to have her routine, she said. She liked to have her snack at eleven, then her walk to the shops or the park, where she was allowed to play in the sandpit but not go down the slide. Didn't I agree that it was too dangerous? And she could not go into the playground at all if there were a lot of rough children there who might push her over. Then she had to come home by half past twelve and have her lunch. Mrs. Maynard would leave it every day in a special place in the fridge and all I had to do was take it out and heat it up. She had to eat it with her own spoon, and then I would sing her some nursery rhymes, and she would have a nap, and then we should play together, and I had to make sure that she didn't touch any electric plugs or fall off the sofa or get too cold. Then, at four o'clock, it would be time for her milk and cookies, and soon after that Mrs. Maynard should be home. Had I understood everything? Would I like her to run through it all over again? She had written some notes for me on this piece of paper. Perhaps they would be enough.

At long last she picked up her bag and actually got herself out the front door. But I wasn't at all surprised to hear the key in the lock two minutes later.

"The potty! I forgot about the potty!" she said, and then she had to show me where it was kept, neatly tucked under the sink in the bathroom, and explain the sign Jackie used when she needed it.

At last she had gone.

For a few minutes I did nothing. I just sat there, enjoying the peace and the lovely feeling of being in charge. It made me think all over again of that red dawn when Ben was born. Then a clock chimed somewhere, and I jumped to my feet. It was eleven o'clock already. Time for Jackie's snack. I couldn't afford to let the routine slip only five minutes into Day One.

I'd been all nervous before I started the job, worried that I'd gotten rusty looking after a child, but after that first day, when I seemed to be running in circles to keep to Mrs. Maynard's precious routine and was worried anyway about doing everything right and remembering all the instructions, I found I slipped into it as easy as winking. There was no point, of course, in pretending that Jackie was Ben. She wasn't. She never would be. She could never begin to take his place. Even so, although I told myself all the time that she wasn't the same, I still kept on falling into the trap of expecting her to do the same kinds of things. But in every way, Jackie was miles ahead of Ben. She could walk, for one thing, and use the potty (though she forgot it sometimes) and ask for what she wanted by pointing to it, though she couldn't say a word. She could do other clever things, too, like singing along with me in a wordless hum when I sang to her.

It didn't take me long to realize that Jackie had been spoiled and coddled since the day she was born. Mrs. Maynard was so frightened that she might do herself an injury that Jackie had never been allowed to do anything by herself. She wouldn't try to go up and down stairs by herself, or climb onto a chair, or turn on a tap. She'd stand at the top of the steps going down to the street from the apartment and wait patiently till I was ready, then she'd put out her arms and expect to be carried down. No wonder Mrs. Maynard looked exhausted so much of the time. Jackie was small for a four-year-old, but she was still a tidy weight. I realized, too, that Mrs. Maynard was in the habit of waiting on Jackie hand and foot. She hadn't even tried to teach her to put her own socks on or to wash her own hands.

It was realizing that that made me ambitious. Jackie, I was sure, was capable of much more than Mrs. Maynard realized. I began to think out a plan of all the things I could teach her. I wouldn't tell Mrs. Maynard. I'd surprise her when Jackie had learned something really spectacular, like brushing her own hair.

Mind you, I began to regret after a while that I'd started on hair. On my first two days, Jackie had stood quite still, as good as a doll, waiting for me to do it for her. But after that I didn't let her get away with it. She had to join in the whole operation with me. The trouble was, I had no idea that hair was so difficult. Ben had never gotten near being able to cope with that kind of thing, so it was all new ground for me. I began to see how many different things you do when you do your hair, like holding the brush so that the bristles are pointing down and then pulling it in the right direction. And when you've done one side, you've got to start all over again on the other side without messing up the bit you've done. Incredibly complicated. Think it out sometime. You'll see what I mean.

I tried first just showing Jackie how I did my own hair. That didn't take me very far. She couldn't concentrate for more than a couple of seconds at a time. Then I put the brush in her hand and sort of stroked her head.

"Jackie do it," I said. She smiled at me, her little pink tongue as ever poking out from between her teeth, but without the faintest sign of comprehension.

"Jackie do her own hair," I said again and, dropping on my knees in front of her, I put the brush into her hand and curled her fingers around it. Then together we pulled it through her hair. She roared with laughter. This was a lovely new game, but she had no idea what I was getting at.

"Look," I said, and I did it again. "Now Jackie do it."

After five minutes I thought we'd done enough for one day. Anyway, I was getting bored, and so was Jackie. I dressed her, carried her downstairs, found the stroller, strapped her in it, and went off to the shops. I was dying to show her off to Mrs. Chapman.

I was so busy steering the stroller and worrying about Jackie dropping her teddy on the pavement (Mrs. Maynard had very strict views on hygiene) that I almost walked straight past Debbie without seeing her. She came up behind me and touched my arm.

"So this is your famous summer job, is it?" she said, looking at Jackie. She sounded sarcastic. I had obviously caught her on a bad day.

"Yes, this is Jackie," I said, looking down with pride and checking quickly that her nose didn't need a wipe. "Isn't she gorgeous?"

"Matter of taste, I suppose," said Debbie.

I looked up, shocked. I'd forgotten how awful Debbie could be. She'd been so nice to me over Ben that I'd gotten sort of lulled into a false sense of security. But perhaps I was tougher now than I'd been a couple of years ago, or perhaps I'd just learned a thing or two from Katy. Anyway, I stopped myself from rushing full-tilt to Jackie's defense and said, "How's your job going?"

"I haven't got one," said Debbie flatly. She didn't say any more, but I knew, because Miranda had told me, that she'd tried, and failed, to get taken on by a couple of boutiques. It was the only kind of summer job she'd consider doing, she'd been heard to say grandly, because most other kinds of temporary work were so demeaning.

"Serves you right for being so choosy," I wanted to say, and was surprised at myself. I hadn't even thought of criticizing Debbie before. She went on down the road, and I looked after her, wondering for the millionth time how she managed to walk without the slightest bottom wiggle at all, when a thought suddenly struck me. Debbie was still just as beautiful, of course, but in a kind of way that I could see, for the first time, wasn't very attractive. When you looked at her, you could tell that she'd spent hours ironing out every last crease on her blouse and more hours still scraping every last hair off her legs, but the result was almost too perfect. It made her seem cold. Miranda didn't have a straight nose or wonderful hair or huge eyes, and she looked like a crumpled mess most of the time, but she had warmth and sexiness dripping off the ends of her fingers.

"Poor old Debbie," I suddenly thought as I realized that in spite of all her airs and graces she'd never had a proper boyfriend.

As usual I talked to Mrs. Chapman about it when Jackie and I finally got to her shop, after an expensive and time-consuming ten minutes at the ice-cream truck, which I knew Mrs. Maynard wouldn't approve of. Mrs. Chapman wasn't a gossip, because she never passed tidbits on, but she had this kind of thirst to hear about other people's lives. It was how she built up her phenomenal knowledge of human nature, I suppose.

"I knew someone like your Debbie once," she said. "Skin like eggshell she had, and lovely long white hands. She was so pretty she'd have made a beautiful calendar, hanging on the wall there. Funny thing was, though, she never got married. Boys used to turn around and whistle and all that, but give them five minutes of her high and mighty talk and they'd be off. She went on being beautiful till she was a poor old girl like me. Had a passion for cats. Looked lovely, they did, curled up on her lap. Seems a shame, though, doesn't it? A waste of all them good looks, if you ask me."

I thought about Debbie on and off for the rest of the day. It was as if a spell had been broken. I'd been groveling all these years, never sticking up for myself, always feeling grateful for the slightest crumbs of attention, and here I was, free at last, not caring anymore whether she was nice to me or not.

"There's more to friendship than that," I thought, and way down at the bottom of my mind was an irritating whisper, which I tried to smother: "Perhaps Mom was right about her after all. She does need her bottom smacked."

I didn't tell Mrs. Maynard about the progress we were making with the hair. For one thing, I wanted to give her a surprise. For another, we were going so slowly. Every day I spent longer and longer at it, guiding Jackie's fingers, showing her, talking, encouraging, until in the end she really began to cotton on. And once she'd started, she got the idea quicker than I'd ever expected. One minute she was standing there, breathing heavily, fingers working cumbersomely, tongue sticking out farther and farther, and the next minute she'd made a proper stroke and then another and then another. She'd done it!

She knew at once that she'd been a clever girl. She clapped and laughed and wriggled with pleasure. I was so pleased, I picked her up and danced about with her in my arms.

"Clever Jackie! Brilliant Jackie! Clever little girl!" I sang to her. I was making so much noise I didn't hear the front door open and shut, and when I did hear someone come into the room behind me, I'd got my hair all tangled up in the buckle on Jackie's dungarees and couldn't look up. I couldn't wait, though, to tell Mrs. Maynard the news.

"You'll never guess what," I said, busy with my hair, "clever Jackie's learned to brush her hair all by herself, haven't you, my love?"

There was no answer. I got myself untangled and turned to look at Mrs. Maynard. But it wasn't Mrs. Maynard.

In the doorway stood Tony.

Fifteen

————

Iт's ONE THING TO DECIDE, VERY SENSIBLY, THAT THE PERSON you've been dreaming about for the last year doesn't matter to you anymore, and anyway that you'd rather have someone funny and kind, with bubbly fair hair and an ordinary face. But when you turn around unexpectedly and your daydream is actually standing there, right in front of you, and electric flashes are going off like fireworks, it's another matter, I can tell you. In spite of myself I felt my heart pounding, and it seemed as if an eggbeater had gotten into my stomach.

I'd imagined Tony so much, I suppose I'd built up a false picture in my mind. The real person was shorter, or maybe I'd grown. And although he was good-looking, and pantherish, and all those other things, he didn't have that kind of shining, heroic glow I'd seen around him that first time.

He came into the room and looked at me, frowning. "Where's my mother?" he said. "Who are you?"

"Mrs. Maynard's out," I said. My voice started on a

kind of squeak, and I had to cough to cover it up. "I'm here to look after Jackie."

His beautiful black eyebrows plunged down to his nose as he frowned.

"Mother's *out*?" he said. "She never goes out. She's never been known to leave Jacqueline for more than thirty seconds at a time since the day she was born."

"She's taking a course," I said, only able to produce short sentences owing to the tight band that was tied around my chest and was stopping me from breathing. "Word processing. She wants to go back to work."

"Well, well." He dropped the smart leather bag he was carrying and came into the room. Then he looked at me again. The crossness left his face, and the charm suddenly returned. It made me feel weak at the knees.

"Haven't I seen you before?" he said.

"Yes," I said, "last summer at the tennis courts."

He screwed up his face and thought.

"Joe and Barny," he said at last, "and that awful girl who giggles all the time and bites her fingernails."

"Miranda," I said, giggling a bit to myself to think of the hours of wasted passion that Miranda had lavished on the memory of Tony.

He moved into the kitchen, stepping over a pile of toys with which Jackie was quietly playing. He didn't look at her or greet her or anything, and I suddenly realized that Jackie hadn't exactly rushed up to him either. It was odd for her. She usually flung herself at anyone who came to the apartment. The milkman and the postman adored her. They always turned to wave as they went down the street, and she would stand at the window till they were out of sight.

I heard the clink of glasses in the kitchen.

"Hey!" Tony called. "What's your name?"

"Anna."

"Have a drink, Anna. Wine?"

I was terribly embarrassed. For a start I didn't drink usually, and certainly not in the middle of the afternoon. And then I felt it would be all wrong to drink on the job. What if Mrs. Maynard suddenly came home and found me with a glass in my hand? She'd probably give me the sack on the spot. But on the other hand, it seemed silly and childish to refuse.

"Not now, thanks," I mumbled, sounding weak even to myself.

"Come on," he said. "Why not? It'll do you good."

He came back into the living room with a glass in each hand. I took mine and sipped it. Then I put it down behind a potted plant and hoped Tony wouldn't notice. He didn't. He was obviously not a very noticing kind of person. He sat down on the sofa, crossed his legs, and stretched one arm out along the back.

"How did you meet my mother?" he said.

Perhaps it was the way he said the word "mother," or perhaps it was something in his face, or perhaps it was my famous sixth sense that told me he and Mrs. Maynard didn't hit it off too well.

"I've got a Saturday job in a shop," I said, pleased to find that my voice was under control at last. "Your mother advertised there for a baby-sitter, and I answered the ad. I've often seen her coming in with Jackie, and Jackie and I had gotten to be friends."

I looked over quickly to make sure Jackie was all right. She had put something into her mouth. I went over and fished it out. It was a paper clip. Mrs. Maynard would have had a fit. I looked around, found the box she'd taken it out of, and moved it to a higher shelf. According to the timetable, I should have been playing with her at the moment, but she seemed quite happy on her own. Anyway, I couldn't possibly concentrate on playing with Jackie since Tony had arrived. I was beginning to relax a bit. My heart was just about beating normally again. The only funny symptom now was a feeling of intense awareness. Everything looked brighter than usual.

I dared to ask a question.

"Are you staying long?"

He laughed.

"What? Here? Not likely. I'm off next week to stay with my dad. He's got a fabulous house in France, and I get to drive around in the Ferrari. Who'd stay here?"

I didn't say anything, but he must have sensed that I was dying to ask a million questions. He shrugged and spread out his hands. He talked perfect English, but he sometimes used a kind of foreign gesture, which made him seem exotic and cosmopolitan.

"Look," he said. "If you want to know about the Maynard family, I'll tell you. My father's English and my mother's Italian. They split up four years ago, and my father's company sent him to France. He makes a lot more money over there than he ever could in this God-awful country. My mother devotes herself all the time to Jacqueline" (I wondered again why he didn't call her by her nickname) "and I am in the middle of a brilliant university career."

He laughed to show that he was teasing and tossed his head back to flick the long mane of hair out of his eyes. The movement made me look away, and I caught sight of the clock. It was nearly four, and Jackie hadn't had her milk and cookies! Mrs. Maynard would be back any minute, and she'd find me neglecting my duties in the middle of a drunken orgy with her son!

I leaped to my feet. I'd taken off my shoes and curled up in a big armchair while we were talking, and in getting up I kicked them right under the sideboard. I had to get down on my hands and knees to fish them out. I was irritated with myself for being so awkward and looking like such a ninny. Tony was so sleek and kind of elegant. I looked crumpled and hot.

I picked up his empty wineglass, fetched out my full one from behind the plant, but with my back between it and Tony so that he couldn't see how little I'd drunk, and carried them through to the kitchen. Jackie followed me. I felt her arms go around my leg and her head cuddle into the side of my jeans. I reached down and picked her up.

"Let's take your cardigan off, shall we?" I said. I'd forgotten how thrilled I'd been about the brushing. It obviously wouldn't interest Tony, and suddenly it seemed much less important to me. Then I only had time to settle Jackie down with her milk, wash and dry the wineglasses, and whisk the bottle out of sight when I heard Mrs. Maynard's key in the lock and her excited voice saying, "Tony!" as she stepped into the living room.

I know you're not supposed to eavesdrop, but I couldn't help overhearing everything from the kitchen. Even if I'd shut the door, I could still have heard through it. I didn't think about it much at the time, but it was a peculiar conversation for a mother and son who hadn't seen each other for three months.

Mrs. Maynard's voice sounded almost nervous: "Are you well, Tony? Are you all right?"

And he sounded bored: "Yes, of course. I've got a pile of stuff here that needs washing." He hadn't got off the sofa or anything to give her a hug and a kiss. He just went on sitting there, with his arm still stretched out along the back. Mom would have said, "Fine, you know where the washing machine is." But Mrs. Maynard only said, "Don't worry, darling. I'll wash it for you."

There's another one that needs his bottom smacked, I thought, and I couldn't help smiling at the thought of Mrs. Maynard putting Tony across her knee.

When I got to work the next morning, Mrs. Maynard was looking harassed. She was hovering anxiously over Jackie, trying to keep her quiet.

"Tony's still asleep," she whispered, with her finger on her lips. "He hates being woken early."

I was envious. I love sleeping in, too, but after about half past eight no one bothers to be quiet in our house. If you want to sleep in, you just have to manage as best you can. The thought of everyone tiptoeing around at half past ten was amazing.

When I went into the kitchen, I could see why Mrs. Maynard looked tired. She'd obviously been busy with the heap of freshly washed clothes that were folded up on the kitchen table.

"Would you like me to iron them?" I asked. Her face brightened.

"Yes, please," she said, "but only when Jackie is taking her nap. She mustn't be running around when the iron is on."

In the end, it was my fault that Tony eventually got up. I was getting Jackie dressed for her daily walk. I was trying so hard to be quiet that I'd picked up the brush and done her hair before I thought about what I was doing. Jackie was furious. She suddenly threw a tantrum and started screaming.

"Shhh!" I said helplessly, "you'll wake Tony!"

His bedroom door opened, and he stood there, all tousled, in his pajamas.

"What the hell's going on?" he said. "Can't you keep her quiet?" Then he saw me.

"Oh, it's you," he said. "Where's my mother?"

"She's gone to college," I said.

He yawned, and then he smiled at me.

"You wouldn't get me some breakfast, would you?" he said. "I'm starving."

Two days earlier, if I'd imagined having the chance of getting Tony his breakfast, I'd have died of bliss. But now that it was actually happening, I wasn't interested. For a start, poor old Jackie was still crying, and she needed to be comforted and to go out for her walk, and then, even worse, I didn't know how to use the elaborate coffee machine that Mrs. Maynard had in her kitchen, and I hadn't seen any instant coffee around the place. Somehow I was sure that Tony wouldn't drink tea for breakfast. Tea's a lot wetter than coffee, if you see what I mean, and Tony was anything but wet.

But at the same time, I didn't like to say no. I mean, I was being paid to look after Jackie, so I thought maybe Mrs. Maynard would expect me to look after Tony, too, like she would herself. Anyway, it was too late to say anything, because Tony had disappeared into the bathroom. So I hastily unscrambled Jackie, who was always easy to pacify, and left her with a cracker while I rushed into the kitchen to put the kettle on and lay out a plate and a knife and some butter and marmalade on the table. It seemed a bit indecent to talk to Tony through the bathroom door, so I just left everything I could think of out on the table and got back to Jackie. She'd made a fine old mess with her cracker, but I decided I'd clean it up when we got home, and we set off at last, me feeling frazzled and Jackie happily following the route we took every day, never bored, always ready to play the same old games of "Boo!" and to smile at everyone she met. That was one thing I never got used to with Jackie. She didn't come as a shock to people in the way that Ben had done. She was obviously handicapped, of course, but she looked appealing too, and she had such a winning smile that most people smiled back at her or even stopped for a chat.

Tony didn't appear at lunchtime. But afterward, when Jackie was having her nap and I was doing his blessed ironing, he sat on the kitchen table watching me and chatted. He looked marvelous. His hair was all moussed into shape, so you could still see the marks of the comb in it, and his clothes were so perfect they could have gone straight into a magazine. He wore them very well too. He'd got his collar turned up at a sort of angle, and his sleeves were rolled back, to look casual, but it must have taken ages to get the look exactly right. For a moment, I wondered how long he'd spent in the bathroom. He certainly didn't throw his clothes on like I did. He had the same effect on me as Debbie always had. I was acutely conscious of dirt under my fingernails and the scuffs on my shoes.

But I could tell he liked me. He liked talking to me, anyway, because he didn't move but stayed on, watching me work around the kitchen, hanging his things up to air or filling the iron with water to make it steam. He talked a lot. He told me about his father's house in France with the swimming pool and the live-in maid, and about the yacht they were going to buy, and he went on for hours about his father's Ferrari, with its special kind of gears or something. I didn't believe half of it, actually, but I liked hearing him talk. It was sort of fantasy, but it was more than I'd ever seen or done, and it was certainly more interesting than ironing. And I enjoyed thinking of how mad with jealousy Miranda would be if she could see me now.

Peace didn't last for long, though. I was ironing a shirt, and like Mom had shown me, I started with the collar. Tony suddenly leaned forward and whisked it off the ironing board.

"Look," he said, irritated, "you've done it all wrong.

Look at these creases down at the points. I wouldn't be seen dead with a collar ironed liked that. This is how you do it."

He took the iron out of my hand and, with infinite care, smoothed out all the tiny creases. I felt humiliated.

"Perhaps you'd better finish it off, then," I said, trying not to sound huffy but not succeeding.

He raised his eyebrows.

"Ironing's hardly a man's job, is it?" he said.

"My dad does it," I said, knowing that I sounded feeble but knowing I was right.

"Oh, he does, does he?" Tony's scorn was unmistakable. I felt suddenly furiously angry. I wasn't being paid to do all Tony's ironing. I didn't mind doing it, but I did mind him taking it for granted that I should. And I minded being criticized very much indeed. Anyway, I was supposed to be looking after Jackie. It was time to get her onto the potty.

"I'll stop there, then," I said. "I've got to get Jackie up now."

"Jackie, Jackie," he said, mimicking my voice. "That's all anyone around here thinks of. What on earth do you all see in her? She should have been put in a home as soon as she was born. She's the cause of all the trouble in this family. She broke up my parents' marriage. Mom couldn't think of anything but her. No wonder Dad got fed up and went off with someone more interesting. I'd have done the same. Everything was fine before Jackie came on the scene. She's smashed this family up. It's so unfair!"

I gaped at him, astonished. The smooth-talking,

grown-up good-looker had gone, and in his place was a child, a small, vain, spoiled child, who was hurt and angry. I felt much older than him all of a sudden. And strangely enough, I liked this Tony more than the other one. He was just like Katy. I could understand him resenting Jackie if she'd broken up his family. After all, poor old Ben could have done the same to us. And Tony had never had a chance to get fond of Jackie. Mrs. Maynard had squeezed him out. He'd never been encouraged to look after her or do things for her and share her, like I'd shared Ben. His dad didn't sound much good, either, with his dumb ideas about men not having anything to do with babies and not being supposed to do the ironing.

I wasn't surprised Tony was so jealous. He'd obviously been the center of his mother's life till Jackie came along, and although Mrs. Maynard tried so hard to please him when he came home, there was no doubt that it was Jackie who now reigned supreme. Mrs. Maynard ran in circles around her, and everyone else came a poor second.

Jealousy was something I could understand. Even though I didn't particularly want to be best friends with Debbie anymore, I still couldn't think of her going off with Emma without a pang. Jealousy was the worst feeling in the world. Poor old Katy had suffered over Ben, too. The difference was, though, that deep down Katy had really loved Ben. Jealousy had sort of gotten in the way of her showing it, but it hadn't stopped her from being sorry when he died and giving him her Bambi. We talked about it sometimes. In fact, Katy and I talked about a lot of things these days. She was turning into a real friend.

Maybe there was hope for Tony yet. Maybe he'd turn into a real friend too.

Sixteen

Tony was actually up when I arrived the next morning. He was drinking a cup of coffee at the table. It was littered with the remains of his breakfast. He never bothered to clean anything up. If I didn't get around to it, Mrs. Maynard did it all when she got home. He looked so sulky, I nearly laughed out loud.

"Morning," I said. "What's the matter with you?" The direct method sometimes works with Katy when she's cross. She can't resist telling you exactly what the matter is. But it failed with Tony.

"Get knotted," he said.

"Okay," I said, and started tying myself in knots, you know, putting my head under one arm and twisting one leg around the other till I looked as if I was in some kind of weird yoga position. He was behaving childishly, so I would too. It worked, anyway. He laughed, a bit grudgingly, but it was still a laugh.

I took another risk.

"You know what," I said. "I think I'd like some of that lovely coffee. Why don't you make me some?"

He looked faintly surprised. He was obviously not used to being asked to do things, particularly in the kitchen. But he got up, meek as a lamb, and ran some hot water from the kettle into the coffeepot.

"You're a funny girl, Anna," he said, looking at me over my shoulder. I felt my heart give a tiny lurch, as if I was on the slippery slope of love again, he looked so handsome. But then he noticed a blob of marmalade that had landed on his spotless trousers, and he was so fussy, sponging it off and inspecting the damage, that it put me right again.

"I'm not funny," I said.

"Yes, you are," he said. "I don't know anyone else like you."

"You can't know many other people, then," I said, feeling vaguely offended.

"No, I don't." He had obviously taken me more seriously than I'd intended. "Don't be deceived by the glittering front I present to the world. I'm a loner."

"Haven't you got tons of friends?" I was surprised. "I thought that at college . . ."

"No," he said, sounding all bitter and cynical. "No tons of friends at college. No real friends at all, in fact. And no bloody family, either. That's life, dear, innocent little Anna. You're on your own, girl. Who cares if you live or die?"

I could tell he was playacting a bit. He was trying to sound dramatic. But he meant some of it too.

"Your mom cares," I said. "She'd do anything for you."

"Used to, you mean." He brought the coffeepot over

and poured some out for me. It was stronger than I liked, but it smelled delicious. He still sounded angry, but he'd dropped the affectation. "If Mom had cared, she'd have tried a bit harder to keep this family together. But she didn't lift a finger to stop Dad going. All she could think about was Jackie. What's Jackie got that I haven't got, I'd like to know? I mean, look at her!"

We both turned to where Jackie was playing. She had put her head down on a cushion and stuck her bottom in the air. She was turning her face from side to side, obviously enjoying the feel of the velvet on her cheeks. She looked so funny, even Tony had to laugh.

"Oh, all right," he said. "I can see she's quite sweet sometimes."

"The trouble is," I said, feeling as if I'd suddenly uncovered a vital truth, "you don't really know her."

"What do you mean?" He looked offended. "How can you *know* a kid like that? She can't even talk."

"No," I said, "but there are lots of other things she can do. She's a real personality. Your mom's spoiled her, that's the problem."

He laughed.

"You don't have to tell me that," he said feelingly.

I didn't say, "She's spoiled you too," but I was tempted. Instead I said, "Jackie could learn to do much more for herself than she does now. Your mom does it all for her."

"What do you mean?" Tony yawned. He was beginning to look bored. I could see he wanted to get back to talking about himself.

"Well, she ought to be learning things like dressing

herself and helping tidy up her toys. You wouldn't believe it, but I've taught her already to brush her own
hair."

"Big deal," said Tony.

"Yes," I said, almost choking on my last mouthful of
coffee. "It is a big deal. It's a huge deal. It's a gigantic
deal. And she's done it."

He was taken aback.

"Okay, okay," he said. "Don't bite me."

But I had to show him.

"Jackie!" I called out to her. "Come here, love. Time
for your walk. Bring your hairbrush."

She trotted obediently into her room, fetched her
brush, and came to stand beside me, one hand on my
knee, smiling up at me expectantly.

I touched her hair.

"Do your hair, Jackie," I said. She giggled and then,
frowning hard, dribbling horribly, she lifted the brush to
her head and began her task.

Tony watched with impatience.

"She's doing it all wrong," he said. He leaned forward to take the brush from her.

I pulled his arm back.

"No! Let her try. You can see what an effort she's
making. Don't take it away from her."

In the silence that followed I could hear the electric
clock above the stove blipping away the seconds and
Jackie breathing heavily through her snuffly nose. Tony
and I were completely absorbed. I stole a look at him. His
fingers were itching to help. His mouth twitched in re-

sponse to each fumbling movement. Like me, he was willing her to do it.

She managed three wobbling strokes down the right side of her head and three more down the left.

"Now the back," I said.

It was the hardest bit of all. The brush wavered through the soft black hair, and then it was done. Jackie gave a crow of joy, threw back her head, and clapped her hands with delight. I heard Tony let his breath out with a whoosh.

He turned to me. "She did it!"

"Well, go on, then," I said. "Tell her how clever she is. She'll understand."

"Clever girl, Jackie," said Tony awkwardly. I had a funny feeling that he'd never really said anything to her before. Jackie was delighted. She wriggled some more, and her tongue stuck out farther than ever.

"Put your tongue in, Jackie." If I told her that once a day, I said it a thousand times. She tucked it back in at once.

"She really seems to know what you're saying." Tony looked astonished.

"Of course she does," I said. "Some things, anyway. Don't try any Shakespeare on her, that's all."

"I don't get it," said Tony. "She wasn't like this last time I was at home."

"Well, how long ago was that?" Tony didn't look thick, but he obviously wasn't all that brilliant.

"Three months, I suppose."

"Well, there you are, then. A lot happens to a four-year-old in three months."

"What else are you going to teach her?" Tony sounded quite enthusiastic.

"I don't know," I said. "She's got an awful lot to learn. I thought perhaps I'd try to get her to put her own jacket on."

Tony looked critically at the jacket.

"Too difficult," he said. "She'd never manage the sleeves. I think you should go for the sandals. They've only got that funny sticky stuff on the straps, you know, Velcro, or whatever it's called. No buckles or anything. They'd be easier."

"Why don't you teach her?" I said.

He drew back at that.

"I'm a man, like I said, not a nanny."

"Silliest thing I ever heard," I said, sounding even to myself like a nursery nurse. "You're a brother, aren't you? You've got a sister, haven't you, and she's alive. You're so lucky, you've got no idea."

I stopped. I could feel myself getting worked up. I knew my face was becoming red.

Tony was looking at me curiously.

"What do you mean?" he said.

"My brother died," I blurted out. "He was much worse than Jackie. He couldn't even walk. But he learned to do a lot of things. And you've got Jackie, and you don't even notice her. I'd give anything in the world to have Ben back again. Anything."

And then, I can't think how I came to be such a fool, but I burst into tears and dashed off to the bathroom. I was there for quite a long time getting control of myself again and then washing my face to make it look less red and splotchy, and flushing the toilet to give the impression that that was all I'd been doing. When I finally came out, I couldn't believe my eyes.

Tony was sitting on the floor beside Jackie (I noticed he'd carefully placed himself on a cushion so as not to get his precious white trousers dirty), holding one of Jackie's shoes. She was looking up at him, smiling, obviously delighted to have his attention, but equally obviously she hadn't got a clue about what he was trying to make her do.

"I thought you said she'd understand." Tony looked up, frowning, and he sounded disappointed. "I've been telling her to put her shoe on for the last five minutes, and she won't do it."

"Yes, but it's like telling someone to make a cake without giving them the recipe," I said. "You've got to show her bit by bit."

I sat down, too, and he gave me the shoe. Then I put it into Jackie's hands and guided it onto her foot. She laughed. It was another lovely new game to her. As soon as I took my hands away, she dropped hers, too, and the shoe fell to the floor.

Tony was ready to give up.

"She'll never do it," he said.

"Yes, she will." I was sure of Jackie now that she'd been so clever with her hair. "Wait and see. We'll do this every day, a few minutes at a time, and she'll get the idea in the end. She can't concentrate for long. It was much harder, getting her to do her hair. You know what? By the time your mom finishes her course, I'm going to have

Jackie doing all sorts of things. I'm going to surprise her with it. Don't let on, will you?"

We both got to our feet. Jackie was already standing by the door, ready to go out.

"Just a minute," I said. "You haven't been on the potty yet."

She squirmed between my legs and made for the bathroom. Tony was going in the same direction. I knew he'd be in there for hours, fussing over his hair and gazing at himself in the mirror.

One day, I thought, I'm going to introduce you to Debbie. You'd suit each other completely. But out loud I said, "Do you mind if we go in first? Jackie will never be able to wait until you've finished."

He laughed. It was funny, but I was really getting to like Tony, in a sisterish kind of way.

Outside the weather had turned. The clouds had blown away, and the sun was out. I was fed up with our usual walk, down to the park and into the playground. On an impulse I turned the stroller and began the long climb up the hill toward the church.

I was winded when I got to the top. I'd have made Jackie walk if she'd been mine. It would have done her good. But Mrs. Maynard was neurotic about roads, and I must say, she did have reason to be. Jackie didn't have the faintest idea about danger. She'd have run in front of a ten-ton truck without a moment's thought.

It was a while since I'd been to church, so I felt a bit embarrassed when Mr. Henderson popped out of the

vestry door and practically bumped into me. I hadn't expected to see him there.

"Hi, Anna!" He bent down and poked Jackie in the
tummy. "Hey! Who are you?"

"She's Jackie." I felt suddenly proud of her. "I'm
looking after her."

"Good for you," he said. I could see he was thinking
of saying something embarrassing, about Ben, or about
me being specially fit for this kind of job, but he didn't
say anything. Mr. Henderson could be very tactful.

"We've missed you at the club," he said.

"I'm sorry . . ." I began in a rush, feeling around
for an excuse and not finding one.

"Don't be sorry." He interrupted me with a smile.
"Just come on Friday. They've organized a disco. Over
my dead body, I said, but they insisted. Jeff asked me
what had happened to you."

"Are you sure he meant me?" I asked. I didn't want
to be had twice.

"Well, he said Anna Peacock and asked for your
phone number. I gave it to him. I hope you don't mind.
He said he'd call you this evening."

I couldn't help it, but I got that dumb sort of kick-
in-the-stomach feeling again.

You idiot, I told myself sternly. You only stopped
thinking about Tony yesterday. But I knew it wasn't a
question of love. It was more a feeling of something exciting about to happen, and of a new, more confident me,
a hundred years older than I'd been a year ago. A thousand times wiser.

"Mustn't hold you up," said Mr. Henderson, opening the door of the graveyard for the stroller. "I suppose you've come to visit Ben's grave."

I hadn't, but I went in anyway. It was the first time I'd dared come since the funeral. I don't know why, but I hadn't wanted to. The idea of it had sort of upset me. Mom came regularly, I knew, and tidied it up and planted flowers and things. But I'd always made an excuse not to go with her.

It took me a minute or two to find it, but there it was at last, under an old oak tree in the corner of the cemetery. The stone said simply,

Benedict Peacock
Aged 2 years

A ripple of wind ran through the long grass at the edge of the field beyond the hedge and ruffled the leaves. It blew Jackie's scarf across her face, and she wriggled to be let out of the stroller. I undid the strap and she struggled free then, feeling playful after being held down for so long. She started to run around, peeping out at me from behind the gravestones, clambering onto chunks of granite and sliding clumsily off them again, pointing and laughing at marble angels.

"No, Jackie," I started to say, "not here." It seemed disrespectful to the dead somehow, to use the graveyard as a playground. But then I thought of Ben in my dream, swimming free and happy, strong and supple, away into the middle of the lake, and I let her play. Ben wouldn't have minded, I was quite sure of that. He'd have tried to follow her, getting his dungarees muddy and laughing every time she whisked her sweet little monkey face around to wave at him.

ABOUT THE AUTHOR

Elizabeth Laird was born in New Zealand. Her family moved to England when she was three, and she was educated there. She studied languages at Bristol University and at Edinburgh University and subsequently taught English in Malaysia, Ethiopia, and India.

She is married to David McDowall, a writer. They have two children, Angus and William.